# His Brother's Child

Pat Ballard

Pearlsong Press
Nashville, TN

His Brother's Child

www.patballard.com



Pearlsong Press
P.O. Box 58065
Nashville, TN 37205
www.pearlsong.com

ISBN: 0-9713247-7-8
Library of Congress Control Number: 2004104468
This book contains the text of the 2001 softcover edition published by Writers Club Press, an imprint of iUniverse.com, with minor revisions.

Other books by Pat Ballard published by Pearlsong Press:

*A Worthy Heir*
*Dangerous Curves Ahead: Short Stories*
*Nobody's Perfect*
*Wanted: One Groom*

To my sisters, Ellen and Jerri,
who “challenged” me to write my first book.

# Chapter 1

**Faith Carr came dully awake.** She was disoriented, lost somewhere in that space between sleep and consciousness. Slowly, she realized she was being gently shaken.

"We're here." A man's deep voice was quietly intruding her slumber-fogged mind.

Suddenly Faith was wide awake and alert, remembering that "here" was in the car with a stranger she now called husband, headed for his home in a state she had never been to.

Through sleep-squinted eyes, Faith took in the large brick house lit by the headlights of the stopped car. She looked questioningly at the man beside her, who had brought her back to the present—where she'd rather not be.

"We're here," he repeated. "We're home." He stepped aside for her to get out of the car, holding the door open for her.

Faith followed the tall stranger up the walk, dreading entering a house she knew nothing of, with a man she'd only met a few days earlier.

He entered the house first and flipped on a light switch just inside the door, lighting up the room before them.

Plush tan carpet covered the floor from wall to wall. The gold-colored drapes flowing from the windows accentuated the carpet and the rich, dark brown leather sofa and loveseat. A large matching recliner with an oversized ottoman filled one corner. An antique table with a lamp stood beside the recliner. She knew without being told that this was where the man beside her spent a lot of time reading.

An arrangement of fresh roses posed gracefully on the antique piano. Everything, including the off-white walls, was done with utmost perfection, and as Faith took in its beauty, admiration glowed on her face. When her glance came back to the man beside her, she realized he was watching her.

"It's beautiful," she said.

"I'm glad you like it. Here's your room." He led her across the living room to a door that opened into a large bedroom that looked inviting and cozy. The same tan carpet covered the floor, but the curtains and matching bedspread were a soft country blue. The bedroom furniture was solid oak and looked brand new. Surely he hadn't gone out and bought furniture for her? One corner of the room had been turned into a cozy reading nook, similar to the one in the living room. Under different circumstances, Faith would have loved this room.

"You have your own bathroom over there." He pointed to a door to her right. "I'll go get your luggage." And he was gone, leaving Faith standing in the middle of the room.

She looked around slowly and wondered what she was doing here. Sudden panic made her long to run from the house. She closed her eyes and clenched her fists. She would go through with this. Now that she had started, she must go through with it.

"Faith? Are you okay?" The man stood in the doorway, loaded with bundles of her luggage, looking anxiously at her.

"Yes. I'm fine," she assured him, as she tried to regain her composure.

He placed her suitcases on the floor. "I think you'll be able to find all the closet space you'll need," he said, before going after the rest of her bags.

When he'd finished unloading her belongings, he started to leave the room, then turned back. "If you need anything during the night, even if it's just to talk, I'm down the hall, on the left. Just call me." He smiled, trying to reassure her.

Faith watched him softly close the door. She took the door lock and turned it ever so slowly, trying not to make any noise. She didn't know the man stood on the other side of the door, or that he smiled faintly when he heard the soft grating of the lock.

Feeling too insecure to take a shower, she crawled between the clean sheets on the big, soft bed and curled into the fetal position. What had she done? Why had she allowed this man, this Edward Brenner, to persuade her to marry him? Just because she was pregnant with his brother's child didn't obligate Edward to give the child a name. Why had she allowed her life to get so totally out of her control? Why? Why? *Why*?

**It was almost ten o'clock when Faith woke up the next morning.** She showered and dressed, then set about unpacking and putting her things away. Without realizing it, she was enjoying storing her clothes in the luxurious surroundings.

While she worked, she thought of the man she was now married to. Where was he? No sound came from the other part of the house. Maybe he was still asleep. She dreaded going through the door that separated them, but knew she must. She couldn't hide out in this room until the baby was born.

She took one last look in the mirror. Her thick auburn hair was combed and shining. She had put on just enough eye-shadow to enhance her large brown eyes. She had stopped trying to conceal the spattering of freckles across her nose a long time ago. They were as much a part of her as her auburn hair and brown eyes, and she had accepted that. The only thing she couldn't seem to accept about herself was her weight.

She knew she had come by it honestly. As her parents always used to tell her, "You just take after your aunts and grandmother. You might as well be happy with it. You'll just make yourself sick if you keep dieting like you're doing." But now the dieting didn't even seem to help. She had reached a certain size, and seemed to stay there. She couldn't lose a pound even when she starved herself. And now, her doctor had told her absolutely no dieting while she was pregnant. Of course he admonished her to eat healthily, but no dieting to lose weight.

She slipped into a kelly-green dress that fit loosely. She wasn't showing yet, as she was just a little over two months pregnant, but she felt the dress made her look slimmer.

Finally, not able to find any reason to stay in the room longer, Faith opened the door. She fully expected to see Edward staring back at her, but the living room was vacant. She moved on through the hall into the kitchen, glancing around, openly admiring the beautiful furnishings. Finally, her eyes spotted a note on the table. It must be for her, she reasoned, as she picked it up and read:

> *I've gone to work. Will see you around six o'clock. Just look around and make yourself at home.*
>
> *Edward.*

*Make myself at home,* Faith mused. *I don't even know where I am and I'm supposed to make myself at home.*

*I don't know where I am!* All at once, she felt frightened and lost. She reached quickly for the radio on the kitchen counter and clicked it on. After what seemed like an eternity, the disc jockey finally said, "And that, my friends, is what's happening in Jackson, Mississippi, on this beautiful spring morning."

Jackson, Mississippi? Well, that was one place she hadn't been yet. At least she'd have a new city to explore.

**Faith became aware of the doorbell ringing.** Cautiously, she opened the door to find a middle-aged woman smiling expectantly at her.

"Mrs. Brenner?" the woman asked.

Faith was about to deny the name when she realized that she *was* the person being addressed. "Yes," she acknowledged.

"I'm Beth Cass. I clean the house for Mr. Brenner once a week. Did he tell you I would be here?"

"No, I'm afraid he didn't mention it. But do come in, and do what you usually do. Don't let me get in your way."

Beth Cass came through the door and stopped to look more closely at Faith.

"My, my, you *are* pretty. Where'd Mr. B find you? I knew he'd find a good woman to marry, though. He wasn't never wild like that spoiled brother of his. Poor kid, he's gone now. Was bad, wasn't it?"

Faith hoped the other woman couldn't see the emotions flooding through her. But she didn't have to answer, as the woman continued.

"Oh, sure, I've worked for the Brenners for years. Mr. B's parents used to live here in Jackson, but they bought a big house over in Vicksburg. Yes ma'am, Mr. B and his brother grew up right here in Jackson. I don't see how two brothers could be so different. They've been like that all the time, though. Seems like all that money just made young Frank go wild. Had anything and everything he wanted. The Brenners are just filthy rich, but I guess you already know that since you married one of them." The woman chuckled to herself, and started dusting the furniture. Little did she know she had told Faith more in two minutes than she had learned from Edward Brenner in the past five whirlwind days since she had met him.

She wanted to ask the woman more questions, but decided against it. She couldn't let this old family acquaintance know just how little she knew about the man she'd married.

"Can I help you?" Faith asked instead, not really knowing what she was going to do to pass the day.

"Oh, my goodness, no! You just go and amuse yourself. It won't take me long to do this at all." And she waved Faith off.

"Well, I think I'll walk outside and get a little exercise," Faith mumbled, as much to herself as to the other woman.

"Yes, that's a good idea. You know there's fifty acres that lies back behind this house. Choice property, too. The city's been trying to buy it from Mr. B for several years. They want to build a shopping mall in this area. But Mr. B won't sell. He says it'd be a shame to chop down those beautiful pecan trees out back. And they'd tear down that old barn. Nope, he ain't gonna sell for a while."

The cool spring breeze caressed Faith's face as she stepped out the door. She turned her face toward the breeze and breathed in the fragrance of a bloom she couldn't identify. The scent was heavenly. The happy call of a mockingbird greeted her from one of the many tall, old oak trees surrounding the house. She was amazed at the beautiful lawn and flower gardens that were all around her. Someone spent a lot of time keeping this place looking like a page from *Better Homes & Gardens* magazine.

She made her way around to the back of the house. The oak trees gave way to the stand of pecan trees Beth had spoken of. Faith picked up a few pecans that were still on the ground from the year before and ate them as she slowly walked through the trees, enjoying the tranquility that surrounded her.

Without intentionally doing so, she found herself standing in front of the huge old barn. It didn't look as if it had been used in quite some time, but it still smelled of hay and the animals that had once been there.

Finding an old clump of hay, Faith sat down and looked back at the house. What a wonderful life could be lived here if real love were combined with these surroundings. A child could spend a delightful childhood here.

Faith became acutely, painfully aware of how important true love was to her. A love like her mother and father had shared. Complete togetherness. Everything one of them did, the other one shared, or at least supported. That's why Faith had always been glad they had died together in that plane crash five years ago. She was also glad they didn't know what a mess she'd made of her own life, and how she had come to allow a total stranger to help her make it through the mess.

Faith's thoughts went back to the day Edward Brenner had shown up at her doorstep. She had just finished a crying binge when the doorbell rang. When she opened the door, she was expecting anything except the man who stood before her. His eyes were so blue and vibrant that Faith had felt her heart skip a beat when she looked into them. His face, though clean-shaven, still showed the dark shadow of a heavy beard under the skin, and his hair was coal black, with just a slight tendency to wave. And he was big! He was at least six feet and two or three inches tall, and probably weighed two hundred and thirty or forty pounds. He wasn't handsome in the classic sense, but an overpowering aura of masculinity exuded from him.

"Yes?" she'd asked, wondering what this stranger wanted.

"May I come in?" The voice was strong and confident, with authority sounding in each word.

"I'm not in the habit of asking strangers into my house." Faith couldn't believe he'd even asked the question.

"Are you Faith Carr?" His voice had interrupted her impatient thoughts.

"Yes. I'm Faith Carr, but how do you know my name?"

"I must come in and talk with you." And without waiting for her to consent, he'd pushed past her and walked into her living room.

Faith had been about to insist that he leave when he'd turned that intense gaze on her and asked, "Do you know Frank Brenner?"

Too astonished to speak, Faith had sat down in the nearest chair and allowed the intruder to continue his speech.

"I'm Edward Brenner. I'm Frank's brother. A few weeks ago, Frank came to me after one of his weekend binges, bragging about what he'd done to some woman. He was laughing about how he'd gotten her pregnant. He finally told me her name after several days of coaxing. When I asked what he planned to do about the situation, he just laughed like a madman, and walked out on me. I didn't mention the subject to him again until last week. He shouted at me that he didn't plan to 'do' anything about the situation and he never wanted to hear about it again, and then he stormed from the house. About two hours later, I received a phone call that he had been in a car wreck and was dead." Emotion broke the man's strong voice, but after a brief pause, he continued. "Are you the woman he was referring to?"

"Yes." Faith had almost choked on the admission.

After much persuasion, Edward had finally convinced Faith it would be better for her, and especially for the baby, if she would marry him and give thc baby the family name. He had assured her the marriage would be in name only, and as soon as the baby was born they would get a divorce. But he was determined to see that his brother's child carried the Brenner name, and was well cared for all of its life.

So here she was. In a strange town, married to a stranger who five days ago she didn't even know existed. Could this really be happening to her?

A clap of thunder startled Faith out of her reverie. She had been so involved with her reminiscing she hadn't noticed the dark cloud looming threateningly close. She could see the sheet of rain coming and barely had time to run for shelter inside the barn before it hit.

The scent of old hay and animals from long ago pleasantly surrounded Faith, engulfing her with a feeling of tranquility. She inhaled deeply and looked around her in the dim light.

She was in the middle breezeway that ran through the barn. There were cribs on each side where corn was once stored, and further down the breezeway were stalls where animals had been kept at night. Overhead was the hayloft, which looked like it hadn't been used for many years.

The wind picked up and sheets of rain started blowing in on Faith. She grabbed the handle of one of the crib doors and opened it to step into the dimly lit room, nervously looking around to make sure there were no mice or snakes in the area with her. She heard a faint scuffling in a far corner, but made herself believe it was just the wind blowing through the cracks, rustling an old corn shuck. A flash of lightning illuminated the room long enough for her to confirm there was nothing close enough to cause any alarm.

Faith didn't like storms. She hoped this was just a quick spring storm that would blow over and be gone shortly. The disc jockey hadn't mentioned any weather warnings this morning on the radio, so surely the rain would stop soon.

The rain pounding on the barn's tin roof had a calming effect on Faith's tangled nerves. Even though she was afraid of storms, she could feel a little of the tension she'd carried for the past two months start to drain from her. Maybe this wouldn't be such a bad set-up after all. Edward seemed like such a decent man. As Beth had said, he was so different from his brother. In another life, under different circumstances, she could probably really fall for a man like Edward Brenner.

*Whoa!* Where had that thought come from? Feeling suddenly restless, Faith opened the crib door slightly to see if the rain had slacked off any. Seeing that it had, she was about to step out of the crib when she thought she heard a voice. Quickly pulling the crib door closed, she listened intently. Faintly, in another part of the barn, she could hear what sounded like two men talking. Had they come inside to escape the rain, too? Were they dangerous? Faith's trembling hands held the door closed for fear it would squeak open and expose her hiding place.

As the rain slacked off and Faith could hear better, she could distinctly make out two male voices. They seemed to be enthusiastically discussing business. Finally one of them said, "Okay, we'll meet back here when the next load comes in." Faith could tell by the diminishing voices that they were walking away.

Relieved that they were gone, she stepped out into the main entryway of the barn. Nobody was in sight, so they must have gone in the opposite direction. Faith smiled up at the old hayloft. Soon it would be full of hay again. Surely that's what the man meant when he'd talked about the next load coming in.

Back at the house, Faith was reaching for the door to go inside when it opened before her. "Oh, there you are," Beth exclaimed. "I was worried about you out in this rain, but you're dry. How'd you do that?"

"I took shelter in the barn," Faith explained.

"You didn't see old man Fulton's ghost, did you?" Beth chuckled.

"What do you mean?" Faith felt uneasy, remembering the voices she'd heard.

"Oh, it's nonsense, I'm sure," Beth hastened to explain. "There's a story going around that the old barn is haunted. Several people have reported seeing an eerie light out there sometimes at night. Old man Fulton died out there in the barn when he owned this property. Speculation had it that he might have been murdered, but no one was ever arrested for murder. But you know how people love to get stories like that started. Anyway, I'm finished here. I'll see you next time. I am so glad Edward has found a wife. You be good to him now, he's a fine man." And with a wave, she was gone.

Faith thought briefly about what Beth had said about the old barn being haunted. She didn't believe in ghosts, but she had sure heard voices earlier, and she hadn't seen anyone. An uneasy feeling tugged at her, but she shrugged it off. She would just keep checking and see if that load of hay came in. If it did, she'd know that her voices were real. If no hay showed up—well, she'd only worry about that if it didn't happen.

Faith finished setting the table for dinner at five-thirty. She'd found her way around the kitchen enough to prepare a roast with potatoes, carrots, bell peppers and onions. She had also cooked some green beans and made a salad. Glancing over the table one final time, she concluded that everything looked good.

"Well, it looks like I made pretty good timing, after all," a strange voice interrupted her thoughts.

Startled, Faith whirled to confront the man who had spoken, and immediately disliked him. His eyes were too knowing. His mouth was too childish, and his general look was too smug.

He raked a hand through his blond hair as his smug smile became a little wider. "Well? You got me planted in your memory?"

Trying not to show the fear she felt, Faith asked, "Who are you? And what do you want?"

"What he wants is to stick his nose into other people's business where he isn't wanted," Edward answered from beside Faith. She hadn't heard him come up behind her, but she was weak with relief that he was there.

"Lee, apparently you've heard that I'm married. News travels fast. Meet my wife, Faith. Faith, this is my cousin, Lee Silverhill. Now, Lee, I don't know how you got in here without Faith knowing you were here, but in the future, you'd better knock before entering my house. You could get shot by sneaking up on someone when they aren't expecting you." Faith chilled at the authority in Edward's voice, and she could tell the other man respected it also, even though he tried to pass it off flippantly.

"Yes, Cousin Edward. Just as you say. But your lovely wife needs to keep her doors locked." There was a noted slur in his voice, and Faith glanced anxiously at Edward, who, it seemed, preferred to ignore and forget the whole incident.

"Well, since you're here, and since it looks like Faith has prepared more than enough food for two people, you might as well join us for dinner."

Faith couldn't believe Edward was inviting this insolent intruder to join them.

While they ate, Lee did most of the talking, directing most of his conversation to Faith. Although she tried to ignore him, he acted like he didn't notice, and tried to hold her gaze for long periods of time. She felt too uncomfortable to enjoy the meal she'd prepared and was relieved when he finally made his move to leave.

Just before he reached the door, Lee turned back into the room and, after appraising Faith again, looked at Edward and said, "This thing might work out. You may be able to swing it if you work hard enough, but let me give you just a bit of advice. If you're going to play marriage and make it convincing, you'd better stop acting like you're afraid of each other. Why, Edward, you didn't even kiss your new bride hello when you came home from work. That's kind of unusual for a newly married couple, don't you think? And you practically acted like strangers the entire meal." And with a knowing laugh and a click of the closing door, he was gone.

Faith gasped. "Edward, he knows something! How? Oh, he frightens me!"

"Yes, he must know something. He was part of the bad company my brother was tangled up with. Frank must have told him what happened with you, and Lee must have put it all together and come up with what he thinks is the truth."

"Will he tell anyone?"

"No, I'm sure he won't. He plans to have too much fun tormenting us. Especially you. As long as he's the only one who knows, he can hold it over our heads and enjoy himself greatly."

Faith instinctively knew that for some reason Lee Silverhill was her enemy. She was going to have a lot of trouble out of him. And she dreaded it, because he frightened her more than anyone she had ever known.

"But he's right," Edward added. "If we're going to make people think we're happily married, we've got to act like a married couple. You're going to have to stop acting so shy around me. You know, you wouldn't have married me if you were *that* afraid of me. I know this is going to be hard on you. Especially being pregnant. But like we decided, this is the best thing for you and the baby."

Faith looked into the eyes of the man she'd married to give her baby the security it needed. He'd made a great sacrifice in his life and plans to give his own flesh and blood that same security. He was willing to change everything that was "normal" in his life so another life would have a better chance in this world. She also knew he'd rather die himself than have his parents know their favorite son had been such a scoundrel.

"Wouldn't it be easier for you just to tell your parents the truth? You must have plans of your own. Plans that will be spoiled if you have a wife. Your brother is dead. It can't hurt him now, if the truth comes out."

"That's right. It can't hurt Frank. But it can hurt the people who love him. His parents. There's nothing that's that important to me. When you meet them, you'll understand why I feel this way. They're wonderful, loving human beings, and they don't deserve the hurt they'd feel if they found out Frank seduced you on a drunken dare, then left you pregnant to have and raise his child alone."

# Chapter 2

**Feeling the sharp sting of the memory Edward had just evoked, Faith quickly turned to the table and started cleaning the food away.** Edward started gathering the dishes and carrying them to the sink. When the table was clean, he began running water into the kitchen sink.

"Let's just hand wash them tonight. It'll give us a chance to talk. I didn't mean to upset you when I referred to Frank's bet, but you did know about it, didn't you?"

"Yes, I knew about it. When I called and told him I was pregnant, Frank just laughed at me and said if I was stupid enough to have sex without being on the pill, I deserved to be pregnant. Then he told me he had just 'bedded me on a dare,' because his friends didn't think he'd have sex with a fat woman." Faith tried to hold back the flood of tears that erupted at the remembered hurt and shame, but they came anyway. She buried her face in the cloth she'd been using to dry the dishes.

She didn't resist when Edward pulled her into his arms. Instead, she laid her head against his wide, comforting chest and poured her heart out. "I was so vulnerable the night I met Frank at that party. It was the anniversary of my parents' death and I felt so alone. Frank was so nice and so handsome. Naturally, I felt totally flattered that I, the fat girl at the party, was getting the attention of the best-looking man there. We had a few glasses of wine, and I let him take me home. I can't believe I was naive enough to fall for his line of bull. I'm usually a lot smarter than that." Her tears were slowing down a little now, and she tried to pull away from Edward's arms, even though it felt wonderful to stay just where she was.

"I don't have words to express the horror I feel when I think my little brother could have stooped so low. And to be honest with you, if he hadn't told me the same story before he died, I don't think I'd believe you. He was always a spoiled brat, but he was never mean and hurtful to anyone." Edward's voice was low and comforting.

"Well, I don't put all the blame on him. I was guilty of letting it get out of hand. Although I did try to stop him at the last minute, because I was a virgin, and it dawned on me that I was about to give myself to a total stranger. But by then he wouldn't take no for an answer."

"You were a *whaaat?*" Edward stepped back and gazed down at Faith's tear-blotched face.

"I was a virgin. I know—this day and age women don't usually hang on to that claim until they're twenty-seven, but I've always been self-conscious about my weight and didn't think a man would want me, so I haven't dated much. Plus, I've always thought abstinence was the best way to prevent pregnancy and disease." Faith broke into a near hysterical laugh. "Yep, that's my luck. Wait all these years to have sex, then the first time I do, I get pregnant." Now her laugh was sounding unnatural.

"Faith! Snap out of it! Don't get crazy on me." Again Edward pulled her into his arms. "Now, you listen to me. First of all, you must not take on a case of guilt from what's happened. Technically, you were raped. If you told Frank no, that you didn't want to go through with sex, and he forced you to anyway, then that is classified as rape. And the other thing is—you have to stop putting yourself down because of your size. You've done that several times in this conversation. You're a beautiful woman. What Frank did and said to you was from his own ignorance, not because of you or your size."

Faith stepped from the shelter of Edward's arms and looked up at him. The beginning of a smile touched her full lips. "Beautiful? I don't think I've ever had that word used on me before."

The look on her face convinced Edward she was sincere. "Well, you might as well get used to it, because you're going to hear a lot more of it," he said, taking the cloth from her hands and blotting the tears from her eyes. "Now, why don't you go on to bed. You're probably still exhausted from the strain of the trip yesterday."

**Later that night, Faith slowly awakened.** Moonlight was shining through the partially opened curtain, flooding her bed with light. She went to the window to adjust the curtain. She could see the old barn from her window, cloaked in moonlight, and remembered Beth's story. She looked at the barn for several minutes, but all she saw was a beautiful old building that spoke of a time gone by when the land around the house was a busy farm.

She was about to close the curtain and go back to bed when she saw the dim glow of a light in the barn's breezeway. She stood still as chills ran up and down her body. Suddenly the light was gone as quickly as she had seen it. Or had she seen it? Was she just imagining things?

She climbed back into bed, scolding herself for getting spooked over a story someone told her. A story that, as far as she knew, had absolutely no truth to it. *But you did hear men talking*, her inner voice whispered as she drifted back to sleep.

The next morning Edward was already gone again when Faith woke up. She hurriedly dressed and ate a quick breakfast. She couldn't wait to go back to the barn. She was going to see if she could find any footprints left from the night before. She'd settle this ghost thing once and for all. If she found footprints, she'd know someone was snooping around the old barn.

The sun was bright, so when Faith entered the breezeway she could see much better than yesterday, when the rain clouds had made it dark and gloomy. She looked at the ground carefully. She could see her footprints from the day before, leading to the crib door where she'd waited for the rain to stop. She went further in, but couldn't seem to find anything that resembled a footprint.

Ignoring the uncomfortable feeling that was trying to invade her consciousness, almost a feeling of being watched, she continued to search for some sign, any kind of proof, that someone had been in the barn the night before. She was positive she hadn't imagined the light she'd seen during the night. Thinking she was going to have to give up without finding anything, Faith looked around one more time. There had to be something!

Then she saw it. A burnt match lay against the side of the wall, almost hidden by a leaf that had blown into the breezeway. A new match. One that hadn't had time to turn dark with age as it lay exposed to the elements.

"Yes!" she whispered as she reached down and picked up the match. This was her proof that *someone* had been in the barn—not *something*. Smiling with accomplishment, she headed back to the house, unaware of the man lying in the loft of the barn watching every move she made.

**When she reached the house, she put the match in her jewelry box.** She didn't know why she was even keeping it, but for some reason, it seemed important to hang onto the match for a while. The person who left it was probably one of the men who was going to put hay in the barn. But why had he been there at night? And didn't he know that a match around an old barn like that could cause a fire that would destroy it all?

On the other hand, maybe it was kids playing around the barn. She would have to tell Edward about the incident. After all, it was on his property. Wouldn't he know it if the barn were going to be used to store hay in? She'd tell him as soon as she had a chance.

"Faith?" As if just thinking about him had summoned him up, he called to her from the living room.

"Hi." Faith smiled timidly as she came from her room. "I was just thinking about you."

"Now that's the way every man would like to be greeted when he comes home from a hard day's work. I hope your thoughts were good ones." His smile was teasing, and Faith felt her heart pound a little faster. His smile was so genuine. It crinkled the corners of his eyes first, then spread to bracket his tantalizing mouth. His teeth weren't perfectly even, but they were white and clean, and Faith wondered how they would feel nibbling on her skin.

Shocked at where her thoughts had ventured, Faith stumbled over her words.

"Uh—huh? Oh, yes, they were." She couldn't bring herself to actually say her thoughts had been good ones, after where they'd just been.

"Were what?" Edward was enjoying the flustered look on her face.

"You know—what you said," Faith stammered.

"I want to hear you say it," Edward persisted. "I want to hear you say you were having good thoughts about me."

"Oh, for Pete's sake, Edward, I'm so confused now, I don't even remember what I was thinking," Faith said, and headed for the kitchen. She had to escape this teasing from Edward. It was new to her, and causing some very strange sensations in the pit of her stomach.

As she started past Edward, he reached out and caught her arm. Turning her to face him, he looked into her eyes. "You look beautiful today, Faith."

Remembering their conversation from the night before, Faith could feel her face burning.

"Please, Edward, don't pity me. You don't have to tell me that just because you feel sorry for me. I appreciate it anyway."

Edward slowly turned Faith toward the mirror hanging on the wall. "Look in the mirror, Faith. Tell me what you see."

"I see a fat person with brown eyes, freckles, and auburn hair," she answered honestly, as she looked into his eyes through the mirror.

"Do you want to know what I see? I see a beautiful, soft woman with the most startling eyes I've ever seen. I know they're brown, but they almost look yellow in some lights. She has hair that's thick and luxurious. She has a mouth that's so sensual a man could spend hours just imagining the pleasures it could bring. She has the most tantalizing little row of freckles across the bridge of her nose, and one day, I plan to kiss every one of them, individually."

Suddenly Edward's face became Frank's and he was once again seducing her, just so he could win a bet. She pulled frantically away from Edward and ran toward the kitchen.

"Faith? What in the hell is wrong with you? Why can't you take a compliment?" Impatience edged Edward's voice.

"I'm sorry, but all of a sudden you were Frank, saying all of those wonderful things he said to me that night." Faith's hands shook with the memory. "And besides that, you said this was going to be a marriage in name only."

"Now, let's get a few things straight right now. I am not my brother. This *is* a marriage in name only, just like we agreed, and I won't lose control and try to force myself on you. But in the event that I should decide to make love to you, you won't ask me to stop, I can guarantee you that." At Faith's sharply indrawn breath, he continued, "And another thing. When I compliment you, I'm sincere. I'm not doing it because I feel sorry for you, or for any other reason except that I'm expressing how I feel. Every day, I'm going to tell you that you're beautiful, and you aren't going to argue with me. In fact, every time I compliment you, I just want you to smile and say,

'Thank you, Edward.' I'm going to teach you how to take a compliment. Are you ready?"

Faith looked at him as if he'd taken leave of his senses. She couldn't believe what he was saying.

"You look beautiful today, Faith." Edward smiled as he spoke the words.

Faith continued to stare at him. Surely he didn't expect her to play this silly little game with him.

"Faith, you know what you're supposed to say."

"Get a grip, Edward. I'm not playing this silly game with you." She couldn't believe he'd seriously think that she would.

"This is not a game. I am very serious. You have one minute to smile and say, 'Thank you, Edward,' or I'll start kissing one freckle at a time until you say it." He moved closer to her, to make good his promise.

"Thank you, Edward," Faith ground out between clenched teeth.

"You didn't smile." He was standing very close to her now. "Say it again and smile."

"Thank you, Edward." Faith's lips trembled as she tried to produce a fake smile.

Edward stared at her lips for a long moment before taking a deep breath and stepping back.

"Now, that's how to take a compliment," he said, then added, "I'm going to cook dinner tonight. You go and amuse yourself. I'll call you when it's ready."

Not wanting to lose another argument, Faith went into the living room. She sat down at the piano and started playing. She played beautifully, going through a string of songs from the present all the way back to the fifties. She was lost in all the memories that playing each song evoked, and had no idea how much time had passed when she looked up and saw Edward leaning on the doorframe with his arms crossed across his chest, listening intently to her play.

"You play exceptionally well," he said.

"Oh, I do okay, I guess—" her voice trailed off when she saw the look in his eyes. "Thank you, Edward," she smiled sweetly, and they both broke into laughter.

"Dinner is ready, m'lady," he said, bowing low, then offering his arm to her. Faith placed her hand on his arm and he led her to a dining room table that was perfectly arranged, even to the candles softly flickering on each side of the floral centerpiece.

Edward pulled a side chair out for Faith and waited for her to sit down before seating himself at the head of the table. The seating arrangement put them intimately close together.

She sat staring at her plate, too overcome with shyness to look at him. When she finally raised her eyes, he was watching her.

"Why are you afraid of me, Faith? How can I help you relax? You're going to get ulcers if you keep on like this."

"I'm really not afraid of you. I—I'm not used to living with a man, and I guess I just don't know how I'm supposed to act in this situation."

Edward reached over and placed his hand over hers, to stop her nervous rearranging of her silverware. She was aware of how large his hand looked covering hers, and the sprinkling of dark hair that shadowed the back and knuckles.

"Look at me, Faith."

The soft strength in his voice and the gentleness in his eyes caused that strange feeling in the pit of her stomach again.

"Please trust me," he implored. "Just be yourself, act naturally, and trust me. I promise I'm not going to hurt you. Do you think you can do that? Will you at least try?"

"I'll try," she promised, even as butterflies swarmed deep within her.

He served the food onto their plates. Faith was amazed at how good it was. He'd prepared roasted chicken, a broccoli and rice casserole, a mixed-bean salad and a green salad. He'd made a frozen yogurt banana split for dessert. He talked the entire time, telling stories about things that had happened on his job as a detective for the police department. He told her he gave a lot of speeches at schools, encouraging kids to stay off drugs. He told her about the many young people he'd helped with their various problems.

Faith realized this man could bring her from tears to laughter within seconds. She also found, to her surprise, that she loved to hear him talk. His slight southern drawl held a caress in its quality, and she felt mesmerized as she sat and listened to him. She had no awareness of how much time had passed until he pointed to the clock and said, "It's ten o'clock. I guess I'd better clean this mess up and call it a night."

"Ten o'clock? Surely not!" Again surprise registered on Faith's face as she checked her wristwatch.

"I'm afraid so," Edward answered, as he stood and headed for the kitchen with a load of dishes.

Faith got up to help clean off the table. She picked up the bowl of bean salad. She'd really enjoyed this evening. Once the initial shyness of the moment had worn off, she'd relaxed and enjoyed herself for the first time in a long, long time.

"What future do you see for us in the beans, m'lady?"

She was so startled by the closeness of his voice behind her that she jumped. The bowl slipped from her hands and would have fallen to the floor had he not reached around her and caught it.

She stood in the circle of his arms with the table wedging her in place. As he leaned around her to set the bowl on the table, Faith realized she could touch his neck with her lips if she wanted to. Dumbfounded at her own thoughts, she became even more acutely aware of the masculine aura that surrounded this man.

Straightening up and moving back only slightly, Edward repeated his question. "Well? What marvelous things did you read in the beans?"

"Oh, the beans!" Faith hastened back to reality. "The beans say that if we don't get this mess cleaned up, we won't ever get to bed." She realized her slip of the tongue as soon as she'd let the words loose.

Edward saw the look of consternation flash across her face. His laugh told her he knew exactly what she was thinking. "Lady, I do believe you have a dirty mind," he said, with a gleam in his eyes.

"I do not!" Faith shot back at him. "It's just that you make me so—you make me think—you—you clean up the damn kitchen. I'm going to bed!"

His laughter followed her to her bedroom door, where she stopped. She hadn't even thanked him for preparing the dinner and for making sure she had such an enjoyable evening. Guilt overcame her previous flare-up of frustration, and she went back to the kitchen.

Edward was leaning over the sink rinsing food out of the dishes, and she could tell he was still slightly smiling. For some reason, the picture he presented jerked at her heartstrings and made her want to put her arms around him and hold him.

As if sensing her presence, Edward looked up directly into her eyes.

"I came back to thank you for making dinner, and for helping me have a good evening. I really did enjoy myself." Her voice and eyes were soft as she spoke.

"Faith?" He was slowly wiping his hands on a drying cloth.

"Good night, Edward. Hurry and go to bed so you can get your sleep," she said, rushing out of the room.

As Faith closed the curtains to her windows, she saw the barn standing in the distant moonlight. She'd forgotten to mention the match to Edward. Oh well, she'd do that tomorrow. She certainly wasn't going back in there tonight.

**The knock on the door brought Faith out of a deep sleep.** Before she could answer, the knock was repeated.

"Wake up, sleepyhead, coffee is ready, and I've made some hot cinnamon rolls. Come on, before they get cold." Edward's voice persisted from the other side of the closed door.

"I have to get dressed first," Faith answered sleepily. She couldn't believe it was morning already. She'd slept straight through the night without waking up even once.

"Just put on your robe and come on, now, I don't like cold cinnamon rolls. Plus, I have to tell you something. It's Saturday, and I've got a special treat planned."

Faith suspected he added the last just to make her curious enough to hurry.

After brushing her hair and washing her face, Faith made her way to the kitchen, which was deserted. Just then, Edward came in through the sliding glass doors that led to the deck.

"Come on out here. I've already got it all set up. It's a glorious day—" His voice trailed off as he stared at Faith's robe. It was a thin, flimsy material, and the outline of her nightgown could be easily seen.

"And the view from in here is pretty good!" The grin on his face was mischievous as he picked up the coffee pot and headed back out to the deck.

Faith stood in the kitchen, where she'd stopped when she first saw him. She was searching frantically in her mind for something else to put on, but she was wearing the only thing she had in the form of a robe.

"Come on, Faith," Edward's voice persisted from the deck.

Not wanting to cause a scene by making him wait any longer, she reluctantly went to him.

A cool breeze greeted her. She breathed it deeply into her lungs. The action expanded her chest, and she looked up to catch Edward's appreciative glance. Quickly, she pulled the robe together and sat down in the nearest chair.

Playing host, Edward brought food and placed it in front of her before pulling a chair close to her and sitting down.

The steaming hot coffee and warm cinnamon rolls were delicious. The glaze on the cinnamon roll adhered instantly to Faith's fingers, and unconsciously, when she finished with the roll, she inserted her index finger into her mouth and slowly licked off the residue of glaze. She was inserting the next finger into her mouth when she looked up and caught the expression on Edward's face. Embarrassed, she grabbed a napkin and hastily started trying to clean the sticky glaze off her fingers, but the paper napkin stuck to the glaze, and when she pulled it away several pieces of napkin stayed on her fingers. Totally embarrassed, she was about to get up to go wash her hands when

Edward pulled his chair close beside hers, placing her almost between his legs.

Faith could feel her heart pound harder as he took her hand and started slowly and deliberately picking off each piece of the stuck napkin. He was so close she could feel the heat from his body as he held her hand and gently turned it carefully to make sure all of the pieces of napkin were removed. When he was finished, he turned her hand over and, looking up to capture her stunned gaze, slowly raised her hand to his lips. As he tenderly kissed her palm, he let his eyes drop to her lips. As if of its own accord, her tongue slowly opened and moistened her lips.

Edward moved as if in a trance as he continued to gaze at her lips and lean slowly toward her.

The sharp ringing of the cordless phone on the table beside them reached their consciousness just before Edward's lips reached Faith's.

He paused only inches from her face, as if contemplating just letting the phone ring. Then, with an irritated moan, he took the phone and spoke a gruff "hello" into the receiver.

"No, Jeff, you didn't wake me up. What's up?"

Seeing her chance to escape, Faith hurriedly stood and went to her room.

Leaning against the closed door, she clasped both hands over her burning face. What had just happened out there? What had she almost *let* happen? Was he really going to kiss her? And would she have let him?

Without waiting for an answer, Faith quickly jumped into a very cool shower. She had to ease her burning skin. After a few minutes under the refreshing water, she started feeling more relaxed and her thinking became more rational.

Edward was just trying to make her feel better about herself, she reasoned. Like telling her she was beautiful. What a joke that was! And making her smile and say "thank you." *What a silly game,* she thought, but couldn't keep the smile off her face just thinking about it.

After dressing in a light-colored maroon pantsuit and putting on a pair of white sandals, Faith couldn't find anything else to keep her in the room, so she headed back to the kitchen to clean up the breakfast dishes. Her pulses quickened at the thought of facing Edward again. Maybe he'd left. She *had* stayed in the shower for a long time.

But to her dismay the kitchen was spotless, and Edward was sitting on a barstool having another cup of coffee.

He flashed her a wicked grin, as if he knew she'd been procrastinating on purpose.

"I thought I was going to have to come and help you finish dressing, it was taking so long." An emotion that Faith didn't recognize flashed in his eyes.

"I was just waiting for you to clean up your mess before I came out here. My mama didn't raise no fool." Faith hoped her quick response covered her sharp intake of breath at the thought of him helping her dress.

"Maybe not, but she sure did raise a beautiful daughter."

"Edward—"

"Say it, Faith." He started to slowly slide off the bar stool as if to come after her.

"Thank you, Edward." Faith burst into a peal of laughter. It felt good to be told she was beautiful, even if he didn't mean it. And it felt good to thank him for it, and pretend he did mean it.

"That's the first time I've ever heard you laugh," he said. "I mean really laugh like you meant it. I like the sound of it. I'm going to see that you laugh more often. That was Jeff Snider who called. He and his wife, Mary, want us to come over and go to a movie with them later on this evening. What do you think?"

Faith felt a sinking in the pit of her stomach. She hadn't given much thought to a social life when she agreed to marry Edward.

Edward saw her hesitation and continued, "You know we can't stay cooped up in this house alone until the baby comes. Although," and again that grin played at the corners of his sensual mouth, "I can think of worse things than being cooped up in a house with you for months."

"Are these good friends of yours?" she asked, trying to ignore the mental images his words had evoked. Faith wondered why he would even want his friends to know he'd married a fat woman. She would have thought he'd try to keep her hidden from his friends as much as possible.

"Yes. They're my best friends. I've known Jeff and Mary for years. They're wonderful people. Look, I'm not going to force you to go anywhere, but the sooner we make our entrance into the real world, the easier it'll get."

"When do you want me to be ready? And what should I wear?" A thought struck her. "Edward, my clothes were okay in my circle of friends, but I'm not so sure they'll pass in your circle."

"What do you mean?" Puzzlement etched lines on Edward's brow.

"Well, it's pretty obvious from this house and from your car and from what Beth said that you have a good bit of money. People with lots of money dress differently than people who just live from paycheck to paycheck. I don't want to embarrass you by looking like I came from the wrong side of the tracks."

"That damn Beth talks too much," Edward said, mild irritation in his voice. "Just wear what you have on. Mary will probably wear jeans and a sweatshirt. That's what she usually lives in." He placed his coffee cup in the dishwasher and turned it on before continuing. "I'm going to run to the office for a few hours, but I'll be back around five o'clock. We'll need to leave around six. Is that okay?"

"Oh, sure, I'll try to be finished with all my chores by then." A hint of derision crept into Faith's voice, causing Edward to glance quickly at her.

"Would you like to come with me? There's not anything to do there, but I guess it'd be a change of scenery." His invitation sounded tempting to Faith, but she declined.

"No, I'll find something to do," she said. She was going to have to find some way to pass the time. She couldn't just become a couch potato until the baby was born. At home, she usually walked four or five days a week with her next-door neighbor. But since she'd been here she hadn't developed an exercise program, and she missed it.

**Six o'clock found them in Edward's car headed for Jeff and Mary's.** Edward looked reckless in a pair of black jeans with a light blue denim shirt tucked into the waist. He wore a lightweight, black leather jacket to guard against the cool spring night. He looked as if he'd just stepped off a motorcycle. Faith wondered what it'd be like to go on a real date with him.

On impulse, Faith said, "You look beautiful tonight, Edward."

She felt the car swerve before he regained control of it and turned to look at her.

Faith couldn't believe what she'd just done, but since she'd started it, she had to see it through.

"Well?" she asked, as he gazed at her.

"Well, what?" he responded, only keeping his eyes on the street enough to keep from wrecking.

"What are you supposed to say?"

He roared with laughter. "Thank you, Faith," he said, then added, "And you look beautiful tonight, too, Faith."

"Thank you, Edward." She smiled at him, actually enjoying playing the game with him. And she did almost feel beautiful tonight. After he'd said that Mary would probably wear jeans, Faith had decided to change into a blue denim jumper with a tan blouse and tan shoes. Her denim jumper was one of her favorite things to wear, so she felt confident in it.

Soon they pulled up in front of a house that had the makings of a mansion. A red convertible sat in the driveway. Another car, a Lincoln Continental, was parked in the garage.

"The convertible's Jeff's," Edward explained. "He thinks it brings out his adventuresome nature. The Lincoln belongs to Mary. She believes in luxury. Jeff and Mary are great jokesters, so be prepared for anything."

As Edward rang the doorbell, he put a protective arm around Faith's shoulders. He knew she was a little nervous at having to meet his long-time friends, under the circumstances. "You'll be fine," he whispered to her in a reassuring voice.

Just then the door was thrown open with a sweeping gesture.

"Well! Look who's here! Come on in. And I guess this is the new bride? Edward, you weren't kidding when you said you'd found yourself a beauty!" The slight touch of gray in the temples of the man's red hair looked out of place on his boyish face. His brown eyes sparkled with mischievousness.

Faith glanced up at Edward, who still had his arm around her. He was grinning at the man in front of them. "Faith," he said, with feigned distress in his voice, "this is the man I call my best friend, so you know I must be desperate for friends. The only thing that keeps this guy afloat is his wife, Mary." Looking around the room, he continued, "Where's Mary?"

"Mary? My Mary? Edward, you know where my Mary is. She's upstairs dressing. She's never, *never* dressed on time. Come on in and sit down. You might as well make yourselves comfortable, because there's no telling how long we'll have to wait. Would you like something to drink? Something to knit? It may take that long. MARY!" he called at the top of his lungs, "THE BRENNERS ARE HERE!"

Faith felt herself start to relax. No worry here. This guy was so busy talking that he'd never notice if she and Edward didn't act like newlyweds. She remembered what Lee Silverhill had said to them about acting like they were afraid of each other. She was sure that's why Edward was sitting so close to her on the sofa, and why he clutched her hand in his as if he'd never let it go. Was he a little nervous, too?

Edward and Jeff struck up an instant conversation about their last golf match and playfully argued about why Edward won, with Jeff accusing him of cheating. Every now and then, Jeff would turn his head toward the stairs and yell, "MARY! HURRY UP!" And each time he did, he'd turn and wink at Faith. She could understand why Edward liked him. He had a most unusual sense of humor.

"Say, Jeff, I've got an idea. When you have to be somewhere on time from now on, why don't you start telling Mary you have to leave an hour earlier than you actually do? Then maybe she'll almost be ready on time."

Edward's suggestion brought an indignant gasp from the direction of the stairs.

"That sounds just like some harebrained Brenner idea! Edward, you stop putting ideas into my husband's head. He's hard enough to get along with as it is. Now 'fess up, Jeff, tell them you told me to take my time. You said there was no hurry."

One of the most beautiful women Faith had ever seen glided down the stairs. She was a true blonde with huge blue eyes. She was tall, probably close to six feet, and came down the stairs with the grace of a runway model. Faith instantly felt clumsy and awkward just being in the same room with her.

She walked directly to Faith and held out her hand.

"So you're Faith. Edward told me he had you. Welcome to our circle of friends. If you want to become a success with all of us, just be good to our Edward. We've all been trying to get him married off for years, but I guess he knew what he wanted after all."

She leaned down and kissed Edward on the cheek. "I have to admit, you did better for yourself than we'd done so far."

Then she turned to Jeff, who had stood up to put his jacket on. She admonished a firm fist to his chest. "And don't yell at me when we have guests!"

Jeff pretended to be mortally hurt. Coughing spasmodically, he led the way to Mary's Lincoln. "Let's take this car. It's big enough for several people to ride in, in case some of the group want to ride together from the theater to the restaurant."

Edward opened the door to the back seat of the car and motioned for Faith to get in. She sat down, expecting him to close the door and walk around to the other side, but realized he was in the process of sitting down beside her. She moved over, but his hand on her arm stopped her from going any further than the center of the seat. After closing his door, he took her hand in his and rested both of them on his thigh, then continued to chat with Jeff and Mary.

He seemed determined to make sure they looked like a newlywed couple, Faith thought. But she had to admit, she loved the way her hand felt, clutched inside his.

Three more couples met them at the theater. After introductions were made, they settled down to watch the movie.

It was an action film with a tender love story intertwined with the action. To make matters worse, Edward seemed determined to either hold her hand or keep his arm on the armrest of her seat close enough to be touching her at all times during the movie. She knew it was just her imagination, but it seemed that he became more attentive to her during the love scenes. Doing things like holding her hand and gently stroking the back of it with his thumb, or leaning over very close and whispering something in her ear. She knew he was just doing it for show, but her pulses responded just as if it were for real. She felt like a teenager out on her first date.

When they left the movie, Faith found herself tucked snuggly under Edward's arm in the back seat of the car as he, Mary and Jeff chatted back and forth. Faith realized they'd been friends for years. Had even gone to school together. She felt like an outsider as she listened to them laugh and talk about things from their past.

Edward was in the middle of a story, with Faith gazing up at him as she listened intently. Unexpectedly, he stopped talking and, placing his hand on the side of her face, slowly lowered his mouth to hers. Her surprised intake of breath parted her lips just enough to allow his tongue to gently caress her top and bottom lip before he ended the kiss. Then in a husky voice he finished his story.

Faith knew he'd only kissed her "because that's what newlyweds do," but she felt the effects long into the night.

# Chapter 3

**Two nights later the phone rang and Faith heard Edward pick up in his bedroom.** She turned her attention back to the book she'd been reading and didn't think anything else about the phone call until Edward came into the living room later.

"That was Dad on the phone. He and Mom want us to come up to see them. They want to meet you. It was a big disappointment when I got married so suddenly and didn't have a formal wedding. They couldn't understand the rush. I explained that since it was so soon after Frank's death, I didn't think a big wedding would be appropriate. Naturally, the entire thing has been kind of a mystery to them. If they hadn't been so involved with their grief over Frank, I'm sure they'd have made me do some real explaining. Anyway, they want us to come and spend a few days with them. Actually, they want us to spend a week, but I told them I didn't know if I could stay away from the office that long."

Faith's insides turned to mush at the thought of spending time with watchful in-laws. Surely they'd be able to guess this marriage was a farce.

"What do you think?" Edward asked. "You know we have to see them sooner or later."

"But a whole week? Will we really be able to fool your parents? Especially for that length of time?"

"Well, we'll just have to put forth our best effort, if you know what I mean," Edward responded, doing his best Groucho Marx imitation. "You wanna start practicing right now?"

Faith couldn't help but laugh at his twitching eyebrows and the pretend flicking of an imaginary cigar. But the laughter didn't erase the tension she felt beginning to mount inside the pit of her stomach.

"We're going to be okay, Faith. They'll love you instantly. And I'm sure they'll be able to understand how I met you and it was love at first sight for both of us, and we didn't want to waste a single moment of our lives by being apart any longer. And that's why we got married so fast."

"Is that what you told them?" Faith wanted to make sure their stories were the same if they were questioned on how they met.

"Precisely. I told them that the moment I saw you, I knew you were the woman of my dreams. The woman I'd waited all these years to find."

"You rubbed it on a little thick, didn't you?" Real concern was in Faith's voice. "If I'm that great, how will they understand it when I have a child and we get a divorce?"

"I'll just tell them you turned out to be a nymphomaniac and were driving me crazy wanting sex all the time, and I just had to get rid of you."

"Yeah, and you dream a lot, too, don't you." Faith couldn't believe he wasn't taking this more seriously. She put her book aside and got up to leave the room. If he didn't want to be serious about this, she'd just go to bed.

"Faith?" His voice stopped her just before she reached her bedroom door.

"What?" she asked, without turning to face him. She didn't know he'd followed her until she felt his hands on her shoulders, turning her around to face him.

"I do dream about you a lot. I dream about kissing you and how good it feels. I dream about holding you in my arms and feeling your soft, warm body close to mine. I dream—"

"Edward!" Her sharp voice stopped him.

"Goodnight, Faith," he said, then kissed the tip of her nose before she turned and fled into her room.

She lay awake long into the night remembering Edward's words and trying to convince herself he'd only said them to try to boost her self-confidence before they made the trip.

**The drive from Jackson to Vicksburg was uneventful.** They'd gotten a late start, so it was dusk when they arrived in the historic town. Edward directed the car into a driveway lined with old oak trees cloaked in drooping gray moss, which led to a huge antebellum home. Faith felt as if she'd gone through a time warp as she gazed at the beautiful old house. Tall, round columns supported a balcony that completely circled the two-storied house.

"Oh! This is beautiful! Simply exotic!" She couldn't find the correct words to describe the grand old house.

"I'm glad you like it. Come on in and meet the folks who live here. I think you'll be equally impressed with them."

Edward, using a key on his key chain, opened the door and let them in. Again, the beauty greeting them caused Faith to stand still to take it all in. They'd stepped into a huge open area. A curved stairway connected the upper rooms of the second floor.

Faith lovingly touched a nearby antique table as she took in the surroundings. The room was decorated in plush bright velvets and smelled of a mixture of time gone by and the present. Thick, soft carpet cradled their footsteps. The place looked like something from a Civil War movie. She expected Scarlet O'Hara to step forward any moment and ask them what they wanted.

"Like it?" Edward asked.

"Oh, Edward. It's beautiful. It's so elegant, yet so comfortable and inviting." Just then, her eyes stopped on a full-length, life-size portrait hanging on the far wall. "Oh!" This time her exclamation was one of stunned surprise, instead of pleasure.

Without being aware of it she moved instinctively closer to Edward, as if he would protect her. Following the direction of her eyes, Edward looked into the lifelike eyes of his brother's portrait. The smile was teasing, friendly, and welcoming, portraying all the charm Frank was so well known for. Edward felt a sudden rush of love and longing for his little brother, as tears filled his eyes. He also felt a tremor go through Faith's body, and knew her emotions were totally different than his. He tightened his grip on her shoulder.

As the couple stood in this position, gazing up at the portrait, a man walked into the room.

"Hello, Son. Isn't that a wonderful likeness of Frank? Looks like he'll speak at any moment." Tears filled the stately man's eyes as he gazed at the face of the son who was lost to him forever.

"But do introduce me." He brought himself back to the couple in front of him and put his arms around Edward. They hugged warmly.

"It's good to see you, Son. And you must be Faith. I liked your name the first time I heard it, and I'm sure I'll love you. You two come on into the library. Mama is reading and she doesn't know you're here."

Faith was amazed at how much Edward looked like his father. Looking at the senior Brenner was looking at Edward in twenty or thirty years. The gray hair and a few added wrinkles were basically the only differences.

They followed him into another large room, where books lined every wall. Soft leather chairs and a couple of sofas invited one to sit and relax.

"Mama," the senior Brenner said to a small woman who looked up from a book in her lap. She could have been an older Doris Day look-alike, and Faith liked her immediately.

"Mama, meet our new daughter, and look how much happier our boy looks. Marriage is agreeing with him, don't you think?"

"Mama" rose from her chair and threw her arms around her son's neck. Overcome with emotion, she didn't speak for a moment, but smiled up into his eyes.

Edward pulled his mother close and kissed her cheek. "Mom, this is Faith, my new wife."

She took Faith's hands in hers, and as their eyes met and held, Faith became more keenly aware of the deceptive life she was leading. This was a wonderful soul standing in front of her, and she suddenly wished she could tell her everything.

"I'm already glad my son married you. I can tell you're good for him. I always prayed he'd find a good woman. I know my Frank would have married a wonderful girl like you, had he been fortunate enough to live." Her voice would not let her go on, and again Edward stepped in.

"Mom, she may be great looking, and she can cook, too, but I sure would love to have some of your coffee and banana bread," he said, hoping to distract her from her line of conversation.

Much later, the two parents led Edward and Faith upstairs. They stopped at a door about midway down a long hallway. "Our room is where it's always been. Just yell if you need anything," his dad told them.

Goodnights were said and the younger couple went into the room they were to share. This was the moment Faith had been dreading. She'd hoped against hope that the room would contain twin beds, but her hopes were dashed when she spotted the large four-poster bed against the far wall. She couldn't hide the concern on her face as she glanced at Edward.

"Don't look so dejected, Faith. Remember I said you could trust me? See that oversized recliner over there? Due to the fact that I can sleep almost anywhere, under almost any conditions, that chair will work just fine as a bed for me." He didn't add that he'd never had to share the room with a beautiful, sexy woman who seemed oblivious to how she affected him.

"You do trust me, don't you?"

His question surprised Faith. She held his gaze for a long moment. Actually, she realized, she *did* trust him completely. "Yes, Edward. I do trust you," she answered quietly.

"I'll go downstairs and read for awhile. That should give you time to do what you need to do to get ready for bed. The bathroom's through that door to your left."

Faith was in the bed and asleep when Edward returned. She never knew when he came back to the room and tried to settle his large frame into the uncomfortable recliner.

**When Faith again opened her eyes, sunlight was sifting through the curtains at the windows.** For a moment she glanced around the room, having forgotten where she was. Then her eyes settled on Edward in the recliner, and she remembered. He looked relaxed, but she wondered if he'd slept well. His present position didn't look very comfortable. She smiled when she remembered that she'd fallen instantly asleep and never knew when he returned to the room. That should answer any questions on her part as to whether she trusted him or not.

He was sleeping in a pair of jogging pants, but didn't have on a shirt. His bare chest was covered in a mass of black, curly hair, and as Faith stared lazily at it she felt her pulses quicken. What would it be like to run her fingers through that hair, and maybe even put her lips on—

A soft knock at the door brought her back to reality with a jolt. If someone came through that door, they'd see the sleeping conditions. Not exactly what a parent would expect of newlyweds.

"Edward!" Faith called softly.

Instantly his eyes flew open. As she pointed at the door, the knock came a little stronger. He was on his feet at once and about to go to the door, when he looked mischievously back at her.

"Just a moment," he called. The wink he gave Faith let her know he'd remembered the situation just in time.

"That's okay, Son. I just wanted to tell you breakfast is almost ready," his father spoke through the door.

Faith, who had been busily scruffing up the opposite side of the bed to make it look like it had been slept in, drew a deep breath of relief and relaxed. Edward grinned at her.

"Close call, huh? You even look beautiful in the morning with your hair all messed up like that." The warm look in his eyes caused Faith's pulses to leap to a faster rhythm.

"Yeah, and sleep must blind you," she responded without thinking.

Before she knew what was happening, Edward was sitting on the bed beside her with her hands pinned behind her head. Only the sheet separated her scantily clad body from his bare chest. She could almost imagine the hair on his chest tickling her bare skin.

"Actually, I see very clearly after I've had a good night's sleep. And what I see this morning is a lusty, sleep-tousled woman who refuses to think anything except the worst about herself." Slowly he lowered his mouth to claim her sleep-swollen lips.

Relaxed and vulnerable from her night's rest, Faith felt herself responding to Edward's kiss. She opened her lips to let him gain more access to her mouth. She was acutely aware of him lowering himself closer to her, and could feel his warm body through the thin sheet that separated them. Emotions she had never experienced before charged through her body. She knew she should stop him, but she seemed powerless to do anything but kiss him back. This was wonderful, and she never wanted him to stop.

His lips left hers and nibbled at her ear lobe, then started working their way down her neck, then lower. Faith moaned with pleasure and turned her face toward the open drapes of the sliding glass doors leading out to the balcony. Through her barely open, passion-hazed eyes, she slowly became aware of the form that stood on the other side of the sliding glass doors, leering at them.

"Edward!" Was that weak-sounding voice really hers?

"Shhhh. Relax and let me make you feel good," he whispered, as he cupped a breast in his large hand.

"Edward." Now her voice was stronger. "We have an audience."

"What?" Finally gaining his attention, she motioned toward the sliding glass doors.

Lee Silverhill stood smirking at them with a knowing look in his bleary eyes. When he saw Edward scowling at him, he saluted and walked away.

Edward's attention came back to Faith. He wanted desperately to continue making love to her since she'd seemed so receptive. He wanted to let her know a man could make love to a woman, but not go all the way until she consented. But that would have to wait awhile. He wanted her to sincerely desire him before he'd consummate their marriage.

The spell had been broken, so he leaned down and gently kissed that vulnerable spot between her breasts, then stood up. "I'll get dressed and wait for you on the balcony."

As Faith lay and listened to Edward stir around in the bathroom, she couldn't believe she'd responded to him like she had. She could feel shame and embarrassment settling over her like a wet, heavy blanket. If she kept acting like she was starved for love and attention, Edward would think she'd willingly led Frank on. He wouldn't believe she'd tried to get him to stop before they actually made love. She buried her head in the pillow and wished she could disappear.

"Faith? *Faith*?" Edward had to walk over to the bed and touch her shoulder before she heard him.

Startled, she turned to him, and he saw the tears in her eyes.

"What's wrong?" Concern was instant in his voice.

"I'm okay." Her answer wasn't convincing even to her.

"No. Tell me what you're crying about. I won't go away until you do. And Mom and Dad are going to get tired of waiting breakfast on us."

"I'm just afraid you're going to get the wrong impression about me because of what happened."

"What on earth are you talking about?"

"You know—when you—when we—when—"

"When I kissed you, and you kissed me back?"

"Yes."

"The only impression I got was that I really enjoyed what we were doing and I can't wait to do it some more." A teasing light danced in his eyes.

"Edward, I'm serious." She tried to reason with him.

"Oh, so am I. In fact, I've never been more serious about anything in my life. Now I'm going to wait for you on the balcony. Hurry, so we can go downstairs and get breakfast. I'm starving, and if I can't have what I want, I might as well eat some eggs." He lightly caressed her cheek with his fingertips before going out to the balcony.

Faith showered and dressed quickly, trying not to think about what had transpired between her and Edward this morning. But she couldn't get it off her mind. She desperately wished her body would stop betraying her every time he was around.

Finally, not being able to find a reason to delay any longer, she stepped through the sliding glass doors onto the balcony. Edward stood looking at the flower gardens below. It seemed to Faith that every species of bird that existed must be singing from the tall, old trees that surrounded the place. Squirrels scampered from limb to limb. The sweet smell of magnolia and honeysuckle, mixed with a faint touch of pine, drifted by on the soft, balmy breeze.

"This is *so* beautiful," she admired, as she walked up beside Edward.

Edward turned to her and was about to speak when a voice from the far end of the balcony interrupted him.

"Well, did you lovebirds finally get up?" Lee Silverhill had come through the sliding glass doors that opened from his bedroom, and was approaching them.

"Good morning, Lee. It's a little early for snakes to be stirring, isn't it? You get your kicks from peeping in other people's windows?" Contempt resounded in Edward's words.

"Aw, now, don't get sore just because I saw you kissing your wife. You practicing for the folks? You've really got them fooled, haven't you? All they can talk about is how wonderful your new wife is, and how happy you look."

Fearing, from the look on Edward's face, that the two men would actually come to blows, Faith took Edward's arm and said, "Come on, Sweetheart, let's go get breakfast."

"You'd best watch your step, Lee. I'm getting real tired of your snide little insinuations," were Edward's parting words as he followed Faith back through their room and down the hall toward the stairs.

Just before they reached the top of the stairs, Edward took Faith's hand in his and turned her to face him. "Sweetheart? Now I really like the sound of that."

"Well, I had to do something. You looked like you were going to jump on him and beat him to death," she answered.

"I may do just that before this is all over," he said, still holding her hand as they approached the stairs.

Just before they began to descend, Edward stopped again. "Don't you think we need to practice again before we go down there? Maybe just one kiss?" He was standing so close that his breath warmly caressed Faith's face.

"Edward—"

"Shhhhhh. Don't look, but I think we have an audience down below. They're waiting for us to come down." He slowly lowered his lips to cover hers as he pulled her close against his massive chest.

Not wanting to appear as if she were rejecting her husband's advances, Faith timidly raised her hands to the back of Edward's head and pulled him closer, fully returning his kiss. Knowing he had initiated the kiss for the sake of the people watching below, she was determined not to end it first. He started this, and he could end it.

"You two lovebirds come on down and get your breakfast," Edward's father called. "You're starving us all to death."

Edward slowly raised his head and looked into Faith's half-closed eyes.

"You taste so good," he whispered for her ears only. "I'd gladly skip breakfast for some more of this."

As they reached Edward's parents below, they discovered Lee had managed to get there before they did.

"Son, it's really good to see you so happy," Edward's father said, as they joined them.

"Thanks, Dad. I feel like I'm finally a complete man, now that I've found Faith. She really is a fine woman." Edward looked at Faith warmly as he spoke to his father. His statement almost seemed believable to her, but she had to remind herself it wasn't true. She glanced over at Lee to find him watching her with open disdain. She felt a cold chill of premonition run up her spine.

They ate breakfast with lighthearted banter going on throughout the entire meal, everyone taking part except Lee. He seemed to enjoy the fact that he was the odd person in the group. He also seemed to enjoy giving Faith much of his unwanted attention and making her feel very ill at ease.

When breakfast was over, Mrs. Brenner looked at Faith and said, "We'll leave these men to do what they want to. I want you to come shopping with me. At the end of the week, probably Thursday night, I want to have a dinner party for some of our special friends so they can meet you. Won't that be grand? And I want you to help me pick out some things for the party."

Faith looked at Edward in desperation. Couldn't something be done to put this party off? Her eyes pleaded with him.

"Mom, are you sure you want to go to all that trouble?"

"Now, Son," spoke Edward's father, "surely you haven't forgotten how much your mother loves to entertain. She'll jump at any reason to throw a party."

"Yes, I do remember, but Faith is kind of bashful around large crowds."

"Oh, we won't let you feel uncomfortable, honey," Mrs. Brenner assured Faith. "We'll make sure you feel at ease and are having fun at all times."

Edward shrugged and said to Faith, "We might as well give up, I think we're outranked on this." His eyes sent her an unspoken apology.

**The day passed quickly.** Faith enjoyed watching Mrs. Brenner spend money. She wondered how it felt to go to the best stores and buy the best items without having to worry about having enough money to pay bills at the end of the month.

Back at the house, they discovered that the men were still out somewhere, so Faith went to her room to rest for a while before dinner. She wished she could tell Mrs. Brenner she was pregnant. She somehow knew the woman would love to know she was going to be a grandmother, but Faith quickly dismissed the idea of telling her as soon as she thought about it.

She was tired from the day and soon dozed off. She didn't know how long she'd been asleep when she came slowly awake. She felt Edward's presence before she opened her eyes to find him sitting on the side of the bed, looking down at her.

"Wake up, Sleeping Beauty. We have to dress for dinner."

"Dress for dinner? Do people still do that?" Her drowsy voice held disbelief.

"Well, I'm afraid my parents, mostly my mother, are trying desperately to hang on to a few of the older customs, and, yes, they still ask that we dress for dinner."

"Is this supposed to be formal wear?" Now she was wide-awake and at full attention. Faith didn't even own a formal outfit.

"No, it's just something besides jeans and T shirts. Not real dressy, but not too casual, either." He stood up, taking Faith's hand and gently pulling her to a sitting position.

"Edward, we have a slight problem, I'm afraid. I've been thinking about this all day. If we're going to be at your parents' dinner party, I'm going to have to buy something appropriate to wear. Otherwise, I'm going to look like I came from the other side of the tracks at this gathering."

"Baby, you could never look like you came from the other side of the tracks."

"Edward, get serious!" Her voice came out harsher than she had meant it to. "By the way your mother spent money today, I *did* come from the other side of the tracks. Haven't you noticed that my clothes aren't the same quality as the circle of people you're around? Haven't you noticed that what I'm wearing has never seen a brand name, and actually, I probably wouldn't even recognize some of the brand names that are in the clothes your people own?"

"I'm sorry," Edward responded quickly, "I didn't mean to sound flippant about your clothes. But, actually, I haven't noticed that your clothes are any different than anyone else's. I don't pay any attention to things like that."

"Well, women pay attention to these things, and I'm sure your mom has noticed. Even though she's much too nice to say anything. But I'm sure she knows your wife didn't come from the same financial background that you did."

"Well, she did mention that you looked like Little Orphan Annie."

"Edward Brenner!" Faith scolded, as he laughed and disappeared into the bathroom to change clothes.

Nothing more was said about shopping for a new dress until the next morning, when, after breakfast, Edward informed his parents, "Faith and I are going shopping today. Faith wants to get a new outfit so she can knock everybody cold at the party Thursday night."

"Well, she could do that in what she has on right now," Mr. Brenner told them with a twinkle in his eyes.

"See what I told you?" Edward whispered to her as they left the room.

Soon Edward pulled the car into a parking space in front of an exclusive-looking dress shop.

"May I help you?" The saleslady made her way to them, never taking her eyes off of Edward.

Faith knew what was coming. She'd visited enough of these dress shops to know they seldom carried clothes in sizes larger than a 10, and not many of that size.

"I'm looking for a gown suitable for a dinner party," Faith said, even though the woman was still looking at Edward for directions.

Looking Faith up and down with a condescending air, the saleslady finally said, "I'm sorry, but we don't carry anything that big."

Faith had been afraid she was going to be embarrassed, trying to shop with Edward along, but she had so hoped they wouldn't run into this kind of attitude in the better shops. She couldn't believe the woman's crass attitude.

Just then an office door in the back of the store opened and a tall, dignified woman came into view. When she spotted Edward she broke into a huge smile. "Edward Brenner! Your mother said you were coming to town."

"Hello, Mamie." Edward took the woman into his arms and gave her a warm hug. She looked to be around his mother's age.

"How are you?" she asked as she stepped back and looked at him closely.

"Well, I'm not real happy right now. I came in here to try to buy my wife a dress, and your salesperson has just been very rude to her."

"Rude? What do you mean?" Alarm was in her voice as she glanced at the stiff-necked saleslady, who was now giving Edward a scorching look.

"This is my wife, Faith." Edward introduced her to Mamie. "Faith, this is Mamie. She and my mother have been friends for years. She owns this store." Then, turning to Mamie, he continued, "We came in here to get Faith a dress to wear to Mom's dinner party Thursday night. I'm sure you and Tom are invited. Anyway, we told your employee, here, what we needed, and she rudely informed my wife that you don't carry clothes big enough for her. Now, I can understand that you may not have clothes in larger sizes, even though I don't understand why you wouldn't, and I can understand that your salesperson would have to tell a customer you don't carry their size, but this person—" here he nodded toward the saleswoman— "this person was mean with her answer and her body language. And I don't appreciate it at all." His voice showed his dissatisfaction.

Mamie turned to the saleslady and said, "June, wait for me in my office, please."

The woman gave Faith another scathing look, then turned and went toward the office door.

Mamie took both of Faith's hands in hers and said, "I'm so sorry. I've had several complaints about June. But this is the last straw. As soon as I'm finished with you, I'm going to fire her. Now, what are you looking for? It's true that we don't stock plus-size clothes in this store, but we have a store across town that's especially for plus-size women. June knows this; she just wanted to give you a hard time. Let's decide what you're looking for and I'll call one of the clerks over at the other store and they can bring some choices over for you."

"We can just go over there," Edward interjected. "You don't need to go to all that trouble."

"Nonsense. I want to do this for you and your beautiful wife. It's so good to see you, Edward. You look so good. Marriage is agreeing with you. Faith, you must be one heck of a woman to capture the elusive Mr. Edward Brenner, and not only capture him, but cause him to look radiant with happiness."

Embarrassed, Faith only smiled at the well-meaning woman.

"Edward, I'm so sorry about Frank," the older woman continued, "He was a good kid. A little wild, but a good kid." Then, not wanting to dwell on a somber note, she smiled and said, "Okay, now what are we looking for?"

A young saleswoman soon arrived with several dresses. After Faith had tried on all of them, she finally settled on one she really loved. The dress was a beautiful shade of teal green. It was very simply made, but it had a look of quiet elegance, and Faith felt like royalty when she had it on. Without realizing it, she hadn't once put herself down for being fat when she looked in the dressing room mirror.

"I'll take this one," she said, coming from the dressing room.

"But I didn't see it on you," Edward said.

"I know. I want it to be a surprise," she answered, with a glow in her eyes.

"Ah, it must really be perfect," Mamie said, with a knowing nod of her head.

When Edward started to pay for the dress, Faith almost fell in a faint when Mamie said, "That'll be two hundred and fifty-five dollars. We'll have the dress sent over this afternoon."

**When Thursday morning arrived, Faith awoke to find that Edward had already gone somewhere.** She was too nervous about the oncoming night to wonder where he was. Could she and Edward fool the people at the party? His parents seemed oblivious to any problems, but would some searching eye discover that all was not as it should be? After all, she'd never been in love, and could only hope she would be convincing enough to everyone.

Anxious and jittery, Faith realized she was pacing the floor of their room. She took a deep breath and reminded herself that this was a party. People would be having fun, not just watching her and Edward. And besides that, so what? This was hers and Edward's life, and not really any of these other people's business.

But she did feel sorry for Edward. Now so many of his friends would know his wife was fat. He must really love his parents to put himself through this humiliation for them. She was realizing more and more that he must be a truly special man.

Her dress had arrived the afternoon before, and every time Faith thought about it, a tingling thrill went through her. It was so beautiful. So "just right." She'd always dreamed of having a dress like this, and having the right occasion to wear it. So she'd made up her mind to enjoy this evening. She wasn't going to put herself down. She was going to pretend she was as beautiful as she felt in this new dress. And if Edward told her tonight that she was beautiful, she was going to believe him. She might not have many occasions to hobnob with wealthy people, so she was going to enjoy herself tonight.

The day passed quickly, and soon it was time to get ready for the dinner party. Edward dressed first and went down to talk with his father and greet any early arrivals. He'd looked stunning in his tuxedo. In fact, the black tuxedo and white shirt had added a dashing, reckless air about him that sent her pulses racing.

Too bad they had to meet under these circumstances. But she knew he'd never notice her under any other circumstances.

Would she have wanted him to? The question leaped at her with no warning. Well, would she?

Faith looked deeply into her own soul and hedged. *Faith, girl, you'd better be very careful here. In this case it'd be disastrous to love your husband. He'll want to be free of you as soon as he can, you know that. Now get your clothes on or you'll be late for your own "get to know the new fake bride" party.*

She slipped into the dress. It was a perfect fit. The neckline dipped just enough to reveal the soft beginning of cleavage. The bodice fit snugly to show off her full breasts, then curved out with her hips to fall in billowy layers that almost touched the floor.

She'd been to Mrs. Brenner's hairdresser earlier today, and her hair highlighted her face in soft, auburn curls. The green dress made her eyes shine like dark pools of mystery.

She hadn't planned to wear any jewelry. The only real piece she had was a pin that had belonged to her mother, and it was in the lockbox in her bank back home. She just couldn't think of putting on costume jewelry with this expensive, beautiful dress.

She became aware of a soft knock on the door, and went to see who was there. "Can I come in?" Edward called softly through the door.

"Yes, I'm dressed."

He stopped abruptly when he caught sight of Faith. It was the first time he'd ever seen her in an outfit that actually showed her body. Everything he'd seen her wear was loose fitting, as if she were trying to hide herself. He'd known when he hugged her that she had curves, but he hadn't realized how well endowed she actually was. He couldn't stop the grin that spread across his face. She was even more beautiful than he had dreamed.

He crossed the room and took something from one of the chest-of-drawers where his clothes were, then came to her. "Turn around and face the mirror."

She did as she was told, and was astonished to see him draping a sparkling diamond necklace around her neck. He took matching earrings from the box and put them on her.

Her pulses raced as she watched Edward's large hands struggle with the jewelry. The heat from his fingers seared her skin when he touched her as he placed the earrings in her ears. She hoped he didn't notice the rapid pulse on her neck. Her heart felt as if it would leap from her throat. She *had* to gain control of her feelings. What on earth was wrong with her?

Finally, Edward's hands stilled, and he rested them on her shoulders. Their eyes met in the mirror. "Can't you see how very beautiful you are, Faith? Look at yourself. If you didn't already have on your lipstick, I would just have to kiss you, right now." Instead, he lowered his head and gently kissed the racing pulse Faith had hoped against hope he wouldn't notice.

She watched his dark head lower and felt his warm lips on her skin. And just for the moment, she believed him. She actually felt beautiful! What a strange sensation.

Then she laughed at herself for becoming conceited. Was Edward brainwashing her? The breathless laugh brought Edward's gaze back to hers.

"Oh, Edward, tonight I do feel beautiful. Thank you for the dress and the jewelry. Thank you for making me feel beautiful."

He turned her to face him, and leaning down, softly kissed one corner of her mouth, then the other. His voice was thick as he said, "We'd better get downstairs. They'll think we decided to stay up here and have a party of our own. And if we don't go now, that just may happen!"

Faith's face glowed with happiness as they joined the guests who had started to arrive.

**Much later, Edward and Faith managed to get a moment to themselves.**

"Mercy! I've met more people tonight than ever before in my whole life," Faith exclaimed, caught up in the excitement of the party. She'd received so many compliments and good wishes that without even realizing it, she was totally relaxed. All of her previous nervous jitters were gone.

"And who said you were afraid of large crowds? You sparkle like the diamonds around your neck. Everyone loves you."

"Everyone?" Faith wished she could take it back as soon as the word escaped her lips. Where had that come from?

Before Edward had a chance to answer, someone tapped him on the shoulder.

"Oh, Edward," came Lee Silverhill's smooth voice. "Look who's here. She's just dying to tell you what she thinks of you."

Faith looked into the cold gray eyes of a woman who looked too elegant to be real. She gave Faith a withering glance, then turned her attention to Edward.

"Edward Brenner! You two-timer! One week we're spending all of our time together, and the next week you're married. Was this a rush job, Darlin'? I'll forgive you if it was. That's what Lee insinuated. But you know, there's always abortion." Her over-accentuated southern drawl oozed out like thick cane syrup on a cold winter morning.

Had Edward really been spending all of his time with this woman? Did he love her? Had he given up his own happiness through a misplaced loyalty to his family? The questions flooded Faith, almost making her lightheaded.

"Faith, I'm introducing you to Lona. You haven't been listening." Edward's voice finally penetrated her question-fogged brain.

"Lona, I'm very glad to meet you," she lied. She was surprised her voice didn't show her irritation at the woman's insinuation that Edward had to marry her. Lee had been spreading his seeds of doubt. Faith knew she'd better be on her guard with this woman. Lona's open hostility was there for everyone to see.

Later, when dinner was finished, the group moved into the large living room. Furniture had been rearranged to make room for dancing.

"May I have the first dance with my wife?" Edward took Faith into his arms even as he asked the question, and they started swaying to the music. The live band the Brenners had hired was exceptional. The Brenners really knew how to throw a party.

"You're a good dancer, Faith." Edward's voice was warm and low. "I think I'm jealous of the person who taught you how to dance like this." He was about to say more when someone tapped him on the shoulder and said, "Cut."

Lee Silverhill's smile was smug as he placed Lona's hand into Edward's. "Thought you might want to recall old times for a little while."

Edward was about to protest, but Lona's arms were already wrapped around him. "Come on, Edward. Don't you want to dance with lil' ole me? We used to dance the night away. Have you forgotten?"

"Well, Mrs. Brenner, want to sit this one out?" The question was self-satisfied. Apparently Lee realized he would be pushing his luck too far if he actually tried to dance with Faith. Without waiting for her answer, he took her by the arm and led her outside to the patio. He continued down the steps and along the walkway until they stopped beside the swimming pool.

"Well, Cousin Faith, how're you enjoying the big-shot lifestyle? Do you fit in? Oh, don't look so shocked. I know Cousin Frank found you in a small, middle-class town over in East Texas."

Faith's temper was boiling. That this slimy creature could stand there with that smug knowing look on his face and talk down to her made her furious.

"I'll tell you what, Darlin', I'll keep your little secret for you under one condition."

"I don't care to hear your conditions," Faith said, turning to walk away. Lee's hand shot out and caught her arm, turning her back to him.

"But you're going to hear my conditions." His breath was hot on her face, his voice low and menacing.

"Lee, come on and dance with me. Edward's gone off and deserted me." Lona's whining voice drifted down to them from the door.

"You'll hear my proposition later," he promised. "Coming, baby." He sent his voice ahead to Lona.

Faith stood beside the pool trying to stop her angry trembling. Slowly, she felt herself calming down. She was having a good time tonight, and she refused to allow this little incident to put a cloud over her evening. She'd deal with Lee Silverhill when the time came.

"Daydreaming?" a soft voice asked behind her. Startled, she turned to find Edward very close. She was relieved to see him. For a moment she'd thought Lee had returned.

"Edward, are you in love with Lona? Wait. I don't have the right to ask that. In fact, I know it's none of my business, but if you are, why did you marry me? I could've survived without you and the Brenner money."

"Is your outburst over?"

When she nodded yes, he continued. "I've never felt anything for Lona except friendship. We've known each other for a long time, but she was closer to Frank than she was to me. When she indicated we'd been spending a lot of time together, she was exaggerating as she usually does. Lona should have been an actress. She spends a lot of energy making things seem like what they aren't. Now, that's enough of that subject." Edward indicated a bench for them to sit on. "Let's sit out here and enjoy this cool spring night, and not talk about anything that's unpleasant, okay?"

Before she could answer, Mr. Brenner called from the door, "Son, your mother wants you for a moment. Can you come here? Faith, he can come right back, I promise."

"Be back in a minute," Edward said, rolling his eyes at his father's interruption.

Was Edward telling the truth? He sounded genuine. But would he tell her if he really were in love with Lona? She didn't think so.

"Waiting for me?"

Faith whirled to face Lee, who was approaching her.

"No, I was not!"

She started to leave, but he stopped her. "*Now*, you'll hear my proposition. If you'll treat me right, no one will ever know what happened between you and Frank."

Faith froze with horror at what Lee was suggesting.

"Oh, now don't go looking all shocked and indignant on me. Frank said you were really a live wire in the sack. He was tempted to go back for more, but he figured you'd try to pin the kid on him, and he didn't want to get involved in that trap. I just want to see if you're really as hot in bed as he said you were."

Faith moved without warning. She shoved him hard and he landed flat on his back in the pool.

The look of pure disbelief on Lee's face just before he went underwater was suddenly hilarious to Faith. Laughing so hard she could hardly walk, she headed for the door to go back to the party inside. She recognized the symptoms of near hysteria, and stopped for a moment to gain control before entering the room as calmly as if the night air had totally refreshed her.

As she stood looking over the crowd, she spotted Edward. He saw her at the same time and made his way toward her. Just before he reached her, Lona stopped him to say something, and they came toward her together.

Faith studied the woman. She looked like someone who got anything she wanted. Did she want Edward? Would she get him in the long run? Probably so, Faith thought gloomily, then briefly wondered why that thought was depressing to her.

"Faith, Lona's looking for Lee. Have you seen him?" Edward asked.

"He was in the vicinity of the pool a little while ago. Maybe he's still there," Faith said, smiling sweetly.

Lona headed for the door that led outside. The band started playing a slow waltz. Edward held his arms open, and Faith went into them.

"I don't trust that mischievous gleam in your eyes, Faith. Have you been into some kind of devilment?"

Faith's laughter bubbled over and rippled through the air.

"Now, what kind of devilment could someone get into at a nice party like this?" she asked innocently.

"I think if I knew the real woman behind those eyes, I'd be afraid to answer that."

Just then a small commotion came from the doorway to the patio. Faith and Edward looked around to see Lee standing there, dripping water all over the floor. His blond hair clung bang-fashion to his forehead. Water flowed from the top of his head down his body, puddling around his shoes. He glowered coldly at Faith. The dancers had stopped in their tracks to stare at the soaked man, an astonished Lona beside him.

He glared at Faith. When he spoke, his voice was barely controlled fury.

"Mrs. Brenner, that was a cute trick you played on me. Now, I have a few tricks that I'll play in my own good time.

# Chapter 4

**The dinner party had broken up quickly after Lee's dramatic entrance.** The guests had been considerate, knowing that something was wrong, and said their goodnights and left. Edward was downstairs reassuring his parents that all was well, and that Lee and Faith had briefly had a few cross words.

But soon Faith heard them ascending the stairs, coming down the hallway. Edward stopped at the door and said good night to his parents before entering the room.

Faith had started toward the door when he entered. "Shouldn't I apologize to your parents?" she asked.

"For what? Lee's the one who should be apologizing. Now I want to hear what happened. Talk to me."

"You know when you came out to the pool and found me? Lee had asked me to go out there and talk with him while you and Lona danced. Well, he made a real nuisance of himself, then Lona came and asked him to dance—"

"Whoa!" he interrupted, holding up both hands to stop her. "What do you mean he made a nuisance of himself?"

"He said if I would be good to him, my secret would be safe."

"That son of a bitch!" Edward exploded. Faith feared his parents would think they were fighting.

"Well? Then what?" He was waiting for her to continue.

"He—he—repeated some things Frank supposedly told him about me." She felt her face burning hot just remembering what Lee had said, and she prayed Edward wouldn't insist she repeat them. She hurried on with her story. "He was standing so close to the pool, and I was so angry that I didn't even try to keep from shoving him in. I just shoved him and ran."

She expected anything but the loud laugh that escaped Edward's throat. But it was short-lived.

"The utter gall of the cheap bastard! I ought to drown him, not just shove him in a swimming pool."

"Then you aren't angry with me for upsetting your parents' party?"

"Angry? Faith, don't ever let him talk to you like that again. Not ever! But next time, maybe you'd better come and get me. I'd rather he take his revenge out on me."

"Do you think he'll tell?"

"I don't think he will. As long as he knows he has something to hold over your head, he feels like he's in control and can keep us guessing what he's up to."

Faith sighed deeply, resting her face in her hands. What a day! What would Lee try next?

Edward's voice interrupted her thoughts. "You're tired. Tired of being on the alert all the time. Go to bed and try to rest. We'll go home tomorrow."

Home. That sounded so good to Faith.

**Edward went back downstairs to try to unwind and relax a little.** That might give Faith a chance to have some time alone. He could sense her tension.

She'd had a wonderful night. He'd watched her closely and could tell she was enjoying herself, then it had to end on a negative note. He didn't know how much longer he'd be able to put up with Lee's shenanigans. He might just have to tell his parents the truth, just to thwart Lee's little game.

He hadn't made Faith repeat what Lee had said to her, because he had a feeling that he knew. Frank had painted a very clear picture of the night he and Faith had spent together. Edward wouldn't dare embarrass her by making her repeat the things he felt sure Lee had said to her. Damn him, anyway. Edward couldn't see why his parents liked Lee so much.

**Faith was still awake when Edward came back to the room.** She was swiftly developing a headache. She had her back to the door, though, and pretended sleep. He went into the bathroom and put on a pair of the jogging pants that he slept in every night. When he returned, he sat in the big recliner that had been his bed for a week.

Faith knew he must be tired of not having a real bed to sleep in. She heard him let out a long sigh, but wasn't expecting his voice to shatter the quiet of the room.

"Why aren't you asleep? You aren't still worrying, are you?"

Startled by his voice, she turned to face him.

"What makes you think I wasn't asleep?" she asked.

"You weren't in the position you usually sleep in. Your breathing wasn't deep and relaxed. Now, what's wrong? If it's what happened tonight, forget it."

"Okay," Faith agreed, and turned her back to him again. The more she tried to relax and go to sleep, the worse the pain in her head became.

How long she lay there trying to talk herself into sleep, she didn't know. Maybe if she washed her face, she'd feel better. Hoping against hope that Edward had fallen asleep, she cautiously turned her face and looked straight into his watchful eyes.

"Would it help to talk?" His voice was gentle with concern.

Faith shook her head, then changed her mind. Maybe it would help to talk a little.

"I'm not worrying. I have a headache. It's nothing bad, but I've been having them a lot lately."

"You haven't mentioned it."

"Why would I?"

"Because I might be able to help. It's probably tension. Turn over on your stomach," he said, getting up and coming to her.

Faith shook her head. "No, it'll be fine. I'll go to sleep in a minute."

"Turn over."

Faith resented the authority in his voice, but did as he said. He began to very gently massage her neck and shoulders, yet used enough pressure to instantly start working magic on her tense muscles. She was amazed at how powerful his hands were. She had a brief mental flash of those hands on other parts of her body, but was too weary to dwell on those thoughts. She felt herself slipping, slipping, and soon she was fast asleep.

She never knew when Edward stooped and kissed her hair. She never knew that as he sat back down in his recliner and watched her slow breathing, he repeated the wedding vows, this time with their meaning etched deeply into his heart, knowing that he would always love her, protect her, and cherish her above all others, and that he would always be there for her, for better or for worse.

**The next day they said good-bye to Edward's parents and headed back to Jackson.** They'd ridden quietly for some time when Edward said, "Faith, we have to tell them you're pregnant. We don't want them to be able to guess by looking at you, do we?"

"I guess you're right. I suppose you should tell them the next time you talk to them, huh?" She dreaded the fuss the older couple would make when they knew they'd have a grandchild. She'd feel even guiltier about the lie she was living when they knew she was pregnant.

"Why so quiet?" He interrupted her thoughts.

"Oh, I was just thinking if it's hard now to live this lie, how much harder it'll be when they find out they'll be grandparents. Edward, you were right. Your parents are adorable, and I hate that we have to deceive them."

"Why can't you just pretend the baby's mine, and stop worrying about deceiving them? You and I are married and we're going to have a baby. Let's just dwell on that and not think about anything else right now."

If only it were that easy. But her future was unsure, and she had to think about it occasionally.

"Where did you grow up?" Edward asked, changing the subject.

"All over. Dad's job carried him from state to state. I was born in South Carolina and lived there a year. But we'd been in Texas for two years when Mom and Dad had their accident. I've lived in Massachusetts, Colorado, Texas, Ohio, and even in Canada for a while. I went to twenty different schools. That's about my life's history."

"That's a pretty busy one. It sounds like you were very close to your parents."

"Yes, very. Dad and Mom were in agreement that where he went, we all went. Mama said a family wasn't a family unless it was together. She would have gone with him to the ends of the earth and back." Emotion shook her voice as she spoke of the two people she missed so much.

"Could you ever love a man that much?" He took his eyes off the road long enough to look questioningly at Faith.

She resented the question, but answered anyway. "I'll probably never have the chance to find out. Not many men want to marry a fat divorcee with a child." She didn't quite conceal the tinge of sadness in her voice.

"There you go again, delving into the negatives. Why can't you believe positive things can happen to you?"

"Like what? Like my parents dying an untimely death at an early age, leaving me alone? Like me just once trusting the wonderfully kind words of a stranger, and winding up pregnant? You tell me what positive things in my life would cause me to believe that everything's going to wind up rosy." Cynicism was now apparent in her voice, and she was close to tears.

"Well, I kind of hoped you might find me somewhere in that category."

"Oh, Edward! I'm *so* sorry." Faith reached out and placed her hand on his arm. A keen thrill shot through her as she felt the strength of the rippling muscles that lay beneath her fingertips. "Yes, you're the one good thing that has happened to me in a long time. I still can't believe how you've laid down your own life for your brother's child. Most men would have run as far away as they could from this situation. Please forgive me for not acting more appreciative toward you." As she talked, without realizing it, her fingers were gently stroking his arm in small circular motions.

Edward reveled in the thought that she felt at ease enough with him to be unconsciously stroking him. If she only knew the direction his thoughts were continually going, she'd think he was worse than his brother. He had to constantly fight his growing hunger to make love to her.

"Edward! Look at that storm cloud! Have you noticed it?"

He wasn't sure, but her voice seemed close to panic. "Yes, I've been watching it for a little while. It does look kind of fierce, doesn't it? Maybe I'd better turn on the radio and see if they're saying anything about it." He didn't want to alarm her more than she already appeared to be, but he was sure they were in for a strong storm. Maybe a bad one.

Several songs came over the air before a voice interrupted saying, "We repeat the previous weather report. Severely strong winds, dangerous lightning, and possible hail will be moving through our area until four o'clock. Stay tuned for further reports."

"I don't think we need further notice, from the looks of things." Edward clicked the radio off just as a strong gust of wind rocked the car. A flash of lightning split the sky, to be applauded by a crashing clap of thunder, and then the rain hit.

The rain was so heavy Faith couldn't see the highway in front of the car. She glanced at Edward, who was leaning over the steering wheel, straining to see the road. Even with the wipers on high, the road was almost indistinguishable.

"This is too dangerous to drive in," he decided out loud, and pulled slowly over to the shoulder of the highway.

Faith glanced at him. He smiled to reassure her, but she didn't feel any better.

"Afraid of bad weather?" he asked, turning the engine off, but leaving the headlights on dim.

"How bad?" she responded, trying to sound braver than she felt. Just then another flash of lightning ripped across the sky, and the hands that quickly popped over her ears belied her remark.

The car seemed to shudder in the strong wind. Faith could imagine them becoming airborne at any moment. An eerie darkness had surrounded them .

Suddenly a flash of lightning seemed to crash to the ground just outside Faith's door. Terrified, she moved quickly away from the door, welcoming Edward's arms as they came around her. She hid her face on his shoulder.

The storm raged on outside. Faith was sure she'd never experienced such a severe thunderstorm in her life. She wondered if it would ever stop. She felt ashamed for trembling and being such a coward.

"Don't be afraid, sweetheart, we'll be fine. It's just one of those really fierce southern storms that hits with a blast, then quickly moves on."

His deep, strong voice had a comforting effect on Faith. In fact, as she became aware of being in his arms with her head pressed against his chest, she realized that she *did* feel safe, almost as if the storm couldn't reach her as long as he held her close.

And, suddenly, she wished she never had to leave his arms again. How wonderful it would be to know she really belonged to Edward and he belonged to her, and that he would always be there to protect her.

*Great*, she scolded herself. All she needed was to fall in love with the man who was just living for the day he could be rid of her.

Slowly, to her horror, the truth crept unwanted into her awareness. She was in love with Edward Brenner! Stunned at this new revelation, she drew slowly back from him so she could look into his face.

The lightning flashed fiercely and repeatedly outside the car, but Faith wasn't aware now of the storm going on around her. There was a greater storm raging within her very being. All she was aware of was the face that had suddenly become so dear to her, etched in the eerie glow of the lightning.

Edward looked down at Faith as she drew back from him. He was expecting some comment on the storm, but she only stared at him. Her head was tilted slightly to one side and her lips were gently parted. He didn't try to fight his desire as his lips lowered to cover hers.

Here, in the shelter of the storm, with no one to see them, Faith knew Edward was kissing her because he wanted to. There was no one to impress. No one to convince that their marriage was real. For the first time in a long time she didn't question what was happening. She just allowed herself to feel the emotions swirling inside her. She slowly slipped her arms around his neck and pulled him closer to her. Oh, to have this moment last forever!

Edward felt intoxicated with the feel of Faith's lips returning his kiss and her soft, willing body within his arms, yielding and pressing into him. He wanted to make love to her so much he ached, but now wasn't the time. Not now, when she was vulnerable with fear from the storm. If he did, he'd be no different than his brother, and Faith would resent him just as she did Frank. But, oh, she felt good. He slid a hand cautiously up and ever-so-gently cupped a breast. He felt her small gasp, and she pressed into him even closer. If he didn't stop now he wouldn't be able to, and if he did *anything* to destroy her confidence, she might be lost to him forever.

So, slowly, he took his lips from hers. But instead of releasing her, he pulled her close and hard against him, wishing he never had to let her go.

As desperately as she wanted to stay close and sheltered, Faith pulled reluctantly back and looked once again into Edward's eyes. Her throat ached to tell him of her newly discovered love for him. Instead, she said in a shaken voice, "We'd better go, hadn't we?"

Edward's voice was low and husky when he tried to talk, "Faith, I—"

She placed a soft finger on his lips to stop him. "Please don't say anything right now." She couldn't bear to hear him apologize or say he didn't mean the kiss. She just wanted to revel in the feel of his strong arms holding her close and his lips claiming hers as if he had every right to do so.

As she moved back to her side of the big car, Edward started the engine and eased back onto the highway.

Nothing was said as both rode with their own thoughts, watching the thunderstorm slowly drizzle itself away until the sun was once again beaming down on them.

After driving in silence for a while, Edward exited off the interstate and pulled into a small restaurant. "Are you hungry?" he asked, looking tenderly at her.

She gazed deeply into his eyes. Her heart pounded a little harder with the knowledge of the secret she now held close. How long had she loved him? Since the day he knocked on her door and invited himself into her life? Or was it a few days later, when she stood in front of the minister and promised to love and cherish him forever? Did she know even then that the words she spoke were true? Or had she loved him all of her life? Right now, that's how it seemed.

She wanted to reach out and caress his cheek, but instead she nodded yes to his question and reached to open the car door.

"Faith." Edward stopped her with his hand on her arm. He took a tissue from a box in the back seat and leaned toward Faith. Before she could ask what he was doing, he started gently cleaning off the lipstick that had smeared around her lips as they'd kissed. His actions were almost as exciting to Faith as the kiss had been. She could feel her pulses quicken as he carefully surrounded her lower lip with the tissue, then moved to the top lip. As he worked with his right hand, his left hand was entwined in her hair to hold her head still. When he finished, he slowly lowered his hand from her hair and let it trail lazily down her arm until he captured her hand in his.

"I liked that flavor," he whispered softly, as if he'd been reliving the kiss while he removed the telltale signs. "Was it strawberry?"

"Raspberry," Faith managed to squeak out. She felt as if her chest would explode from her pounding heart.

Edward raised her hand to his lips and, turning it over, kissed her palm. She heard her own sharply indrawn breath as she felt the light touch of his tongue on her tender skin.

"We'd better go inside," he said, getting out of the car quickly. Before Faith could get her door open, his hand was already on the handle opening it for her.

When they had finished their meal and were on their way again, Faith asked, "Did you notice the man in the corner by the window?"

"No, I have to admit, my mind wasn't exactly on another man. And it doesn't do much for my ego to think you were watching some other man," Edward joked.

"Oh, be serious," Faith retorted. "He gave me a weird feeling. He had long hair and a mustache, but I just felt like—oh, that's stupid, it couldn't have been."

"Couldn't have been what?" Edward's curiosity was up.

"Nothing. I'm just imagining things."

"Faith, I'd like to know what you started to say."

"Well, I just had the most uncanny feeling that the man was Lee Silverhill. I know it's a silly thought," she ended, feeling embarrassed.

Because she sounded so sincere, Edward didn't have the heart to tell her the idea was, indeed, farfetched. Wasn't it?

What was Lee's means of support? He never worked, and yet he was always loaded with money. Was he in some kind of shady business? He'd been suspicious of Lee for some time now, but why would he be in a restaurant along the interstate dressed in disguise? Edward scolded himself for sounding as jittery as Faith.

**When they reached home, Faith busied herself unpacking her clothes, then went into the kitchen to get a drink of water.** She found Edward standing in the middle of the kitchen holding a piece of paper.

"What does this mean, Faith?" he asked, coming to stand beside her.

He held out the piece of paper for her to look at. There was a sketch on the paper. It looked like a rough drawing of the old hay barn. At the bottom of the sketch two words were written: KEEP AWAY.

"Do you know anything about this? It sure seems to be a warning to someone. It was hanging on the screen door. It looks like someone was trying to draw a barn. Could it be the barn out back?" He seemed to be talking to himself more than to Faith, so she didn't bother answering.

"Oh, well," he shrugged, "probably just some kids playing around."

She still hadn't told him about the match she'd found, and the men she'd heard talking, or the light she'd seen that night. Well, apparently this wasn't the work of a ghost. But why had someone left a warning note? It surely must have been for her, since she didn't think Edward had been out to the barn lately.

She knew she should tell him about the incident, but suddenly she felt excited about exploring the situation further. If she could get the answers to what was going on at the barn, she was sure Edward would be impressed with her efforts.

As Faith dressed for bed, she wondered if someone really didn't want her hanging around the barn. Was it just kids playing around? If farmers were going to use the barn to store hay, surely they wouldn't leave a warning note to stay away. Why would farmers care if the owner's wife strolled around the barn? That didn't even make sense!

She dropped off to sleep, still trying to figure out the mystery of the old barn, while Edward, who sat in the living room reading the evening paper, smiled to himself. She hadn't locked the door to her room when she went to bed. It was the first time she'd ever gone into her room for the night without softly turning the lock on the door.

He couldn't keep his mind off that piece of paper. Had it been a warning to them? Had Faith sharply sucked her breath in when she'd read the note, or had that just been his imagination? He'd heard stories about the old hay barn being haunted, but he knew the stories probably came from kids just trying to scare each other. He hadn't used the barn since he bought the place, but he liked to see it standing out there as a reminder of times gone by. It added a nostalgic flavor to his property that he liked. And he was sure Faith hadn't been out there. Why on earth would she want to hang around an old, unused barn?

No, he convinced himself, the note was just left by some neighborhood kids playing around.

**The next morning, as soon as Faith had a chance to get away from the house, she headed for the barn.** She was determined to find out what was going on. If there were a true mystery, she intended to solve it. She knew she should have told Edward about the voices and the light she'd seen that night, and about the match she'd found, but since she hadn't told him already, she might as well see what she could find out before she did tell him.

As she reached the barn she wondered what would be the best method of hiding and waiting to see if someone came around. Where to hide? And how long was she prepared to wait? What a joke! What else did she have to do? If no one showed up today, she'd come back tomorrow and the next day and until they did.

Suddenly, she heard the voices. They were at a distance, but seemed to be getting closer. Her only place to escape was to grab the rickety old ladder propped up against the barn and climb up it into the hayloft. Luckily it held together and she made it to the top. Dust and dry hay particles wafted up to assail her nostrils. She prayed she didn't go into a sneezing fit and give herself away.

Easing further into the interior of the loft, she stopped when she thought she was close to the center. She didn't want to take a chance of making some noise and alerting the intruders of her presence. Lying face down in what little bit of hay was left, Faith found a spot that had a space between the boards wide enough for her to see below. Hopefully, the people with the voices would come close enough for her to see them.

She had barely gotten settled into a spot when she saw three men walking into the breezeway of the barn. They stopped, but they were too far away for Faith to be sure who she was seeing. One of them seemed to be the man in the restaurant—the one she thought was Lee Silverhill. She was *sure* it was the same man. But what was he doing here in Edward's barn?

When he spoke, she knew beyond a shadow of a doubt it was Lee Silverhill. But for some reason he was wearing a disguise. Was it in case Edward saw him on his property? But why had he had it on in the restaurant? Again, was it in case he ran across Edward and Faith, which is exactly what had happened in the restaurant?

"Okay, boys, let's see if John left the last load where I told him to," Lee said, pulling a loose board back and reaching his hand into the space for something.

He pulled out a brown-wrapped package and held it out so the other guys could see it. "Yes!" he declared jubilantly. "Boys, this stuff will bring us a pretty penny when it hits the streets!"

So that's who she'd heard talking when she heard someone say "when the next load comes in." How naive she'd been to think farmers were going to bring hay to the barn.

"Did you leave the warning note for that bitch who's been snooping around here?" Lee was addressing one of the men who was grinning, exposing yellow-stained teeth.

"Yeah, I left the note on the back door while they were up yonder seeing Frank's folks. I'm sure she knows what it was for." After talking a little longer they left the barn, slapping each other on the back and congratulating themselves on a job well done.

Faith couldn't believe what she'd just witnessed. While Edward spent his life trying to help young people stay clean and drug free, this foul cousin of his was making drug deals on his property.

The rest of the day seemed to drag as she waited impatiently for Edward to get home. She was placing their food on the table and thinking about the happenings of the day when a hand caught her arm from behind. Before she could stop herself Faith screamed. Snatching her arm away, she whirled to face her intruder.

Edward stood looking at her with a serious frown on his face. "Faith, you must keep these doors locked. I could have been anyone."

Faith's fright gave way to anger. "Well, I usually do keep the door locked. I just forgot to go lock it when Beth left. But you don't have to frighten me to death just to prove your point!"

"I thought if I frightened you a little, you wouldn't forget again."

"Oh, I'm not likely to forget, after what I saw today."

"What do you mean?"

"I'll tell you when we've finished eating."

"No, you'll tell me *now*. You jumped a little too much just now. You seemed more frightened than the situation called for. Faith, what's happened?" Anxiety filled his voice.

"Remember in the restaurant when I said I thought I saw Lee?"

"Yes?"

"It *was* him."

"How do you know that?"

"I saw the same guy today, with two other sleazy guys, and I think they were picking up some drugs someone had left for them."

"You *what?*" His voice was so loud it hurt her ears. "Where?" he demanded.

"Wait," she interrupted him. "I'll start from the beginning." And she told him everything, from her first visit to the barn, about the light in the barn at night, and the match she found the next day.

When she had finished, his face was deathly white. "Faith, promise me you won't go back there, and that you'll stay here in this house when I'm not here with you. Don't let anyone in, except Beth or me. Promise me, Faith."

"Why?" she asked, puzzled at his apparent fright. Now, *he* seemed to be the one overreacting.

# Chapter 5

**"Why?"** Faith repeated.

Should he tell her? Edward wondered if it would be wise. Why not? She was already more involved than he had wanted her to be. She had every right to know what was going on. Maybe, in knowing, she would be more cautious.

"Okay, Faith. For several months we've been trying to get to the inside of a drug ring that's taking root in Jackson. We know it's here, but we haven't found out who's bringing the stuff in. I had been suspicious Frank was on something before he did what he did to you. He was just different, somehow. I'd even asked him once if he knew anything about a drug ring moving in, but he said he didn't. I don't think he'd have told me anything, even if he knew. But we have to get to the bottom of this if we can. Crime is on the rise, and it may even be gang-related.

"But Lee? I know he's a sorry substitute for a human being. I always hated Frank hanging out with him, because I knew he was a bad influence. But would he stoop to selling drugs? Are you sure it was him?"

"Yes. One of the guys asked him if he thought his cousin's dame would stay away, and Lee asked the man if he'd left the warning, and he assured him he had."

"Damn! There's no getting around that evidence. It had to be him. Faith, you *must* stay away from the barn. And don't breathe a word about this to anyone. Okay?" Concern made his voice raw with emotion.

"Isn't there some way I can help you?" The challenge excited Faith. She wasn't expecting Edward's resounding answer.

"NO! You stay out of this. The less you know, the better off you'll be. Now that Lee has a grudge against you, there's no telling what he'd do if he found out you knew about his dealings in this drug thing. Now, promise me you'll keep out of this."

"Okay, okay. But who's in this with you? Or is that a secret, too?"

"That's a secret, too, I'm afraid. Faith, just forget about this. Just go on as if you'd never seen that little exchange take place."

"Go on as if I knew nothing? When there's top-secret stuff going on in my lap? And when you may be in danger yourself?" Her voice shook on the last question and she turned away from him, hoping he hadn't seen the tears that filled her eyes.

But he had seen the tears. Hope sprang deeply inside him because she cared enough about him to worry.

Suddenly he was behind her, turning her to face him. "Faith, I'm going to be okay. There's no reason for you to worry. Remember, this is my job. I'm trained to do what I'm doing. You aren't. And that fact would put you in grave danger if I allowed you to get involved. Don't you understand that? I'm not only responsible for you, but also for that baby inside you." He placed his hand on her stomach tenderly.

His unexpected tenderness caused a ripple of warmth to flow through Faith, and she swayed slightly toward him. He slowly raised his hand from her stomach to encircle her waist and pull her against him. Again, Faith felt safe and protected in his arms. At that moment, she felt a slight flutter in the center of her universe that caused her to draw her breath in sharply.

"Faith? What's the matter?" Edward held her away from him to look into her eyes.

"The baby just moved. It's doing it a lot now," she said, awe-struck.

"Where?" he asked, putting his hand quickly back on her stomach.

"Here." Faith took his hand in hers and placed it where she'd felt the tiny butterfly flutter in the lower center of her stomach. They realized at the same time that his hand rested in a very intimate spot.

The awareness of his large hand so close to the very core of her being shook Faith with a charge of energy so strong her insides seemed on fire. Their eyes locked, and she knew Edward had seen into her soul.

His head was lowering slowly toward hers when they became aware of the doorbell ringing. Reluctantly, he pulled away from her and went to see who was at the door.

Faith recognized the laughing voices of Jeff and Mary, and went to greet them.

"Ah, there's the beautiful Mrs. Brenner," Jeff said, coming to place a light kiss on her cheek.

"Hello, Faith," Mary said. "I'm so sorry to barge in on you like this. We were passing by, and Jeff insisted that we stop and say hello."

"Oh, that's okay," Faith assured her. "Sit down, and I'll get us something to drink."

"Well, actually, I need to talk with Edward out on the deck." Jeff cut in before Faith could ask them what they'd like to drink.

After the two men left the room, Faith turned to Mary. "Would you like some coffee, or anything?"

"Oh, no, thanks, I'm fine." But she seemed distracted. "Something's up, Faith. Has Edward said anything to you? Jeff is acting as jittery as a long-tailed cat in a room full of rocking chairs. I've been trying to get him to talk to me, but he says there's nothing to tell. They've worked on a lot of cases together, but I think they may be on one this time that's different." Concern sounded in her voice.

Faith desperately wanted to confide in Mary, but she'd promised Edward she wouldn't talk to anyone. So Edward and Jeff worked together. Edward had never mentioned that to her. Why? Was it an innocent slip of his memory, or was there some reason he didn't want her to know they worked together?

"On second thought, I *will* have some coffee if it's made." Mary interrupted Faith's train of thought. They went into the kitchen and sat down at the bar with their coffee. The men soon came to join them.

Edward sat down on the stool next to Faith. He didn't face the bar, but pulled his stool close to hers. Spreading his long legs wide, he pulled her close between his legs, then sat facing her left side as he talked with his friends. His closeness and the intimacy of his position sent blood rushing to her head. For all practical purposes, she was in his arms! If she leaned toward him the slightest bit, her entire left side would press against his chest. She felt as if she might have a stroke at any moment.

As he talked, he seemed to find reasons to touch her. Her hands, her hair—once he reached over and kissed her cheek. *If only he meant it for real*, Faith thought. He was really putting on a good show for his friends, though.

Finally Jeff stood and said they'd better be on their way. Faith was both relieved and disappointed that she would escape the attention she was getting from Edward. She was sure her face would glow in the dark, it felt so flushed.

When they were gone, Faith turned to Edward and asked, "Why didn't you tell me you and Jeff worked together?"

"What did Mary tell you?" Edward's question was quick, and caught Faith off guard.

"Uh, nothing. She just mentioned that you and Jeff worked together, and I was embarrassed to tell her I didn't even know it."

"Faith, what did she tell you?" Now he was close to her, and she would have stepped away from him, but her back was against the kitchen counter.

"Edward! Why are you acting so strange? You're frightening me. She just said Jeff was acting jittery and she was worried about what you two were working on," Faith answered him honestly. "She said it seemed different than usual."

"And what did you tell her?"

"Nothing."

"You aren't lying to me, are you?" He had her face between his hands as he held her head close to his and peered deeply into her eyes.

"No, Edward, I am not lying to you. And I resent the accusation," she hissed through clenched teeth.

"Baby, I'm sorry," he said, releasing her, but still standing close with this hands on her shoulders. "It's just making me crazy with worry to think you might be in danger from that stupid cousin of mine. He knows too much about you. He knows how to hurt you, and me."

"Edward, you're frightening me. You don't think he'd do anything to hurt one of us, do you? I mean physically? Did Jeff tell you something that has you upset?" Fear was making her tremble.

Edward pulled her close against him. "I'm sorry to frighten you. But yes, Jeff had a lot more to add to what we already know. We're getting real close to the people who are bringing the drugs into the city. And it looks like Lee is deeply involved in this. But I don't actually think he would do anything to harm us physically." He'd upset her and now he had to stretch the truth to calm her down. He hated to lie to her because it might make her more careless, but he didn't want her running scared, either. "Just promise me you'll stay out of this, and not talk to anyone, not even Mary, about it."

"But doesn't she have the right to know? Especially if Jeff is in danger?" Faith reasoned.

"Listen carefully to me, Faith. Mary works at the police department. If these thugs had any idea that Jeff was on to them, and if they thought for a moment she knew anything, they'd kidnap her and torture the truth from her. Mary could be in more danger here than any of us. Now you *must* promise me that you will not talk to anyone except me about this." Raw concern edged his voice.

"I promise, Edward," Faith said, finally realizing the situation they were in was very dangerous.

She went to bed that night with an uneasy feeling wedged deeply in the pit of her stomach.

**While dressing the next morning, Faith noticed her clothes were becoming tighter.** Soon she would have to shop for maternity clothes. But she'd put it off a little longer. She was thinking of the child growing inside her more and more now. What would it be? A boy? A girl? Maybe twins? The thought hit her with a jolt. What would life be like, living as a divorcee with a child or children to raise? She knew there were women doing it everywhere, everyday, but she just wasn't ready to deal with that right now. However, the tiny fluttering inside her was becoming more frequent, and she couldn't continue to ignore the fact that there was another life growing deep within her.

When she entered the dining room, she was surprised to find Edward sitting at the table reading the paper.

He glanced up as she entered. "Good morning, beautiful," he said, lowering the paper. He was always surprised at his own response when Faith came into a room. It was like seeing her for the very first time. Almost like that first day she'd opened the door to him and he'd known immediately that he would love this woman.

"You're up early, aren't you?" He watched her warmly as she poured herself a cup of coffee and joined him at the table.

"Early? It's after seven o'clock. That's not early. But what are you doing here?"

"Oh, I just thought I'd hang around and see what my wife does in her spare time."

Faith knew he was kidding with her, but she felt a small tinge of resentment, anyway.

"I promised to be good, didn't I?" She couldn't keep the note of disappointment from her voice. It hurt that he didn't trust her.

"Now don't go and get upset with me, baby. I'm just going to take a few days and hang around here to see if I can spot anything unusual going on. I plan to spend some time out at the barn and see if there's any more traffic going on around there. Didn't you tell me you saw a light one night?"

"Yes, it was late at night."

"I might spend a night out there and see what happens."

Faith couldn't hide the shiver that ran over her body at the thought of spending the night in the barn in the dark.

"What was that all about?" Edward asked.

"Are you really going to stay out there all night with no way to see what's sharing the barn with you?"

"Oh, I'll stay awake. I can hear anyone before they walk up on me."

"I'm not talking about people. I mean—things." Again, she shivered.

"Like what?" Edward sounded confused. "Do you really think the barn's haunted?"

"No!" Faith was almost embarrassed to admit to Edward what she was talking about.

"Then what?" he persisted.

"Well—spiders—and snakes—and mice—and well, just *things*."

Laughter erupted from Edward's throat. He took her hand in his and kissed her fingertips. "You really are all girl, aren't you? I'm glad. That makes me feel like a big macho man who needs to protect his woman!"

Even when he was joking around with her Faith could feel her heart start to pound faster. He had called her his woman! How she longed for him to think seriously of her as his woman.

A mischievous idea occurred to Edward. "I think you need to work on those fears. I think you should come with me. We can take a blanket and spread it out in the loft and lie there all night and listen to the night sounds and just talk and get to know each other. If the bad guys come, then we'll spy on them. If they don't, then we'll have had the chance to spend the night together in a very romantic situation."

"You are kidding, aren't you?" Faith knew he was kidding, but the thought of spending the night with him by her side made her fears diminish slightly. When she was close to Edward, she always felt nothing could harm her.

"No, I'm not kidding, but I don't think you have the nerve to do it." He threw the challenge squarely at her.

"So you think I'm too much of a coward?" Faith would *have* to take him up on his challenge.

"Yes," he said, astounded she was falling for his bait.

"So which night do you want to spend in the barn?" Faith felt perspiration in the palm of her hands, even as she took the challenge.

"Tonight." Edward didn't even hesitate before answering.

"Tonight?" Dismay sounded in her voice. She wouldn't even have time to hope the plans would get changed for some reason.

Edward's deep chuckle brought her eyes back to his. "Now, if you're too afraid, we don't have to do this," he grinned.

"You're really enjoying this, aren't you?" Faith accused. "You're probably just afraid to stay by yourself, so you've tricked me into saying I'd go with you."

"Oh, no," he moaned, "I've been caught in my own trap!" He pretended to hang his head in shame.

When Faith didn't respond, he slowly raised his head enough to peep at her from under a slightly raised eyebrow. She sat staring at him unwaveringly. They both broke into laughter, and Faith playfully smacked Edward on the side of the head and got up to empty her coffee cup.

She was at the sink pouring her cold coffee down the drain when Edward turned her to face him.

"No woman hits me in the head and gets off without paying a price for it." His face was so serious that for a moment Faith thought she'd angered him. Then she saw the twinkle in his eyes. She tried to move away from him, but she was trapped between the counter corner and the refrigerator.

"Oh, no. You aren't going anywhere until you've paid for causing me pain."

"I didn't hurt you! I barely touched you."

"You hurt my pride, so now you pay."

"Oh, so the strong macho man has to protect his pride, huh?" Faith was trying hard to hide the smile tugging at the corners of her mouth.

"Yes, that's about it," he said.

"So what's the price? Let's get it over with." Fake resignation sounded in her voice.

"Don't be in such a hurry. This price is going to have to be paid slowly and seriously."

"How slowly?" Faith thought she could hear her heart pounding in her ears.

"Very slowly. And if you get too fast, you have to start over." His voice was low and gruff with emotion.

"So what is it?" She couldn't stand the suspense anymore.

"You have to pretend that you really want to kiss me, but you aren't sure if I want you to or not. In other words, you have to try to seduce me. And you have to make me believe you're sincere. If I have any doubts, you have to start over. Do you understand the rules?" His eyes held her unbelieving look against her will.

"No, I won't—" Faith tried to escape once again, but Edward's strong arms had her pinned against the counter.

"You have to, or we'll stand here all day." She heard the determination in his voice. Why was he doing this? There was no one around to try to convince their marriage was real. She'd never initiated this kind of thing before, and she was sure she'd make a fool of herself. Her hands shook at the very thought of what Edward wanted her to do.

But at the same time, she realized she really wanted to play this game with him. It *was* just a game with him, wasn't it? Yes, it was just a game. Okay. She could play, too. She'd watched movies and read books. So even though she'd never actually tried to seduce a man, she was sure she could fake it through this little diversion Edward was amusing himself with.

Slowly and gently, Faith started to tug at the tail of the shirt tucked into Edward's pants. Keeping her eyes lowered, watching what she was doing, she pulled until the shirt was sufficiently untucked. Then she reached for the bottom button and undid it. She heard air hiss between Edward's teeth as he sucked in his breath. Carefully and deliberately she opened button after button until she reached his chest and started to expose the expanse of dark curly hair that lay before her. She hesitated only slightly before her trembling hands continued their journey.

When all the buttons were undone, she gently shoved the shirt to each side to expose the full view to her hungry eyes. He was beautiful. Now desire took over her thinking, and she wasn't playing a game any more. She carefully splayed her open hands on his chest and leaned into him, kissing each nipple before slowly kissing her way up to his neck. She kissed both sides of his strong chin before moving to each corner of his mouth. She could hear him sucking for air just before she claimed his mouth with hers in a hungry, consuming kiss that finished knocking the air from his lungs.

Suddenly she was crushed in his strong arms and he was the one in charge. His mouth devoured hers. But then he stopped.

"Okay, it's my turn," he said, reaching for the bottom button of her blouse.

"Edward, no!" Faith didn't recognize the hoarse voice that came from her throat.

"Oh, yes. What's fair for you is fair for me." And his strong hands continued to open the small pearl buttons on the front of her blouse.

Faith had never experienced the sweet thrill of passion that claimed her, body and soul, as Edward's hands undid each button and came in gentle contact with her soft skin. Her black lace bra hooked in the front, and gave no resistance as Edward unhooked the two-clasp closure to expose her large, smooth breasts. Now it was her turn to gasp as he took both breasts in his large hands at once and kissed one, then the other.

But he didn't stop there. Before she knew what he was doing, he took one of the pink tips in his mouth and tugged gently. Faith felt her knees buckle, but Edward supported her with the help of the counter she was pressed against, bending her slightly backwards on it. Then he abandoned where he had been, leaving it cool and moist and lonely. He took the other tip and tugged on it, massaging it gently with his tongue.

She was so sweet. He ached to spend hours exploring her body and making her aware of how she affected him. But if he wanted to prove to her he wasn't a jerk like his brother, he had to stop now, while he still could.

"Faith," he whispered huskily, "we have to stop, or I won't be able to. You are so beautiful, and I want you so badly I ache, but this isn't the time. Not yet."

Faith gazed up at him with blurred eyes. He had said he *wanted* her. And badly! And somehow, she believed him. That was the most beautiful thing he could have said to her. He wanted her. She reached up and laid her hand on his face.

"How did I do?" she asked timidly.

"Oh, baby, you did good." Edward's wide grin lent wings to Faith's spirits.

"How did *I* do?" His question took her by surprise.

"You did very, very good, too," she answered him breathlessly, trying to hold his gaze, but having to lower her eyes from the burning desire in his.

Edward stepped back to let her escape her temporary confinement, but Faith realized now she didn't want to escape.

"I was kidding about us spending the night in the barn. Under different circumstances it could be quite fascinating, but under the present circumstances, I wouldn't put you in that danger."

"If you think it's dangerous, then why are you going to do it?" Faith didn't want him to take any chances.

"I can take care of myself. If you were with me, it'd be harder to escape if danger came too close."

Knowing it wouldn't do any good to argue, Faith shrugged and let the subject drop, but she was still worried.

**Later, as she sat in the den and tried to concentrate on the book she was reading, her mind kept going back to the scene earlier that morning.** Faith was amazed at how she'd responded to Edward. She was amazed at how much she wanted to make love with him. She'd been caught at a weak moment when she gave in to Frank, but what she felt for Edward was something totally different. She knew that difference was love. And oh, how she wanted to show Edward how much she loved him.

She found she could even think about Frank without the self-loathing that had, for a while, swept over her every time she thought about him. She was finding self-forgiveness gradually. Anyone could be weak sometimes. But she knew what Frank had done was termed date rape. Yes, she'd let the situation get out of hand, but then she had tried to back out, and Frank wouldn't take no for an answer. Had he even realized she had been a virgin? Would he have cared if he'd known? She didn't really think so.

She must admit there had been times after she came here that she'd been afraid of Edward. It was nothing he did, just the fact that the same blood ran in his veins that ran in Frank's. *But not the same poison,* she concluded, knowing Frank would have been a different person if she'd met him before he'd gotten involved in drugs.

She knew she would never be afraid of Edward again. There was no fear in perfect love. Her only problem, now, would be to make sure Edward never knew how she felt about him. He was too good a man to have to sacrifice his life to a woman he didn't love and a child that wasn't his.

But he had said he wanted her. She couldn't keep the smile from her face. If a man as handsome and affluent as Edward Brenner could want her, then she must not be all that bad. She knew her feelings about herself had changed forever. From now on, every time self-doubt started to creep in, she'd remind herself that Edward Brenner had said, in a moment of passion, that he wanted her. Knowing he had felt real desire for her was the best boost in her self-image she had ever had.

**Edward spent that night in the barn.** Lee Silverhill and his goons never showed up, but Edward didn't care. He spent the entire night planning his future with Faith. He'd been involved with a few women, but he'd never known one that turned him on as much as Faith did. He felt she was beginning to trust him, and he hoped she was even beginning to love him. And if this morning was any indication, he believed she'd be a perfect match for him sexually.

He could feel his arousal start all over again, just remembering how well she'd played his seduction game. Was she really pretending? And if she were, what would she be like if she was sincerely making love? He groaned and made himself think of something else.

**Faith spent a restless night knowing Edward was in the barn, and possibly in danger.** Just knowing he wasn't in the house made her lonely for him.

As soon as it started getting daylight outside, she got out of bed and went to the kitchen to start breakfast. When Edward came in, he was surprised to find biscuits, eggs, bacon, and hash browns waiting for him.

"You never told me you could cook like this," he said, finishing his last bite.

"You never asked," Faith bantered. "And besides that, you don't need to eat like this every day. It's not that good for you."

"I'll be the judge of that. Now that the secret's out, I'll be whining for this on a more regular basis."

"We'll see," murmured Faith, as she started to clean up the mess.

"Woman, are you challenging me again?" Edward asked, remembering the day before.

"No," she answered quickly, afraid of a replay of yesterday. It'd be impossible to keep her secret from him if they had many more encounters like that.

Edward showered and went to his room to rest awhile. He'd been asleep for a couple of hours when the phone rang.

Faith hurried to answer it so it wouldn't wake Edward, but when she picked the receiver up, he said, "I've got it."

In a few minutes Edward came from his room, rubbing his sleep-deprived eyes.

"What's wrong?" Faith asked.

"That was Jeff. We got a call that the gang we've been trying to catch is moving its operation to Vicksburg. Seems as if they know we're getting too close. I've got to go to the office and meet with Jeff and the others to see if we can come up with a plan. If I could come up with a good enough excuse to stay with my folks without arousing any suspicion on their part, we could go up there so I could stay close on my investigation. But if Lee's involved, and I just showed up in Vicksburg for no reason, I think he'd get suspicious of me." He rubbed his forehead, too tired from his previous night's vigil to try to think this through.

"I've got an idea," Faith offered.

"Forget it, Faith! You're not going to get involved in this."

"Won't you even listen?" she pleaded.

"Okay," he gave in reluctantly. "What's your idea?"

"What if we told your parents that I'm pregnant and having problems, and need to stay in bed for awhile? I'd naturally need someone to help me, and your mother would be the obvious choice. Even Lee couldn't be suspicious of something like that."

Edward stopped rubbing his head and looked unbelievingly at Faith.

"You're a genius! That's the answer!"

# Chapter 6

**"How soon can you be ready to leave for Vicksburg?"** The need for sleep had suddenly left Edward, and he was excited and ready for action.

"By this afternoon," Faith answered, mentally taking stock of what she'd need to do to get ready.

"Great! I'll run down to the office and tell the guys we have a plan. As soon as I can get back, I'll pack and we'll hit the road." He headed for the door.

"Are you going to let your parents know?"

"Oh, yeah," he said sheepishly, and went to the phone to make the call.

Later that afternoon, in the car headed to Vicksburg, Edward let out a long, low moan.

"What's wrong?" Faith asked.

"I just remembered the recliner. I'll die a slow death if I have to sleep in that recliner for an indefinite length of time." He moaned again for effect.

"I thought you said you could sleep anywhere." Faith reminded him of their first trip to see his parents.

"Yes, but that was when I thought it'd just be a few nights. We may be talking a month or more, at this point." The dread in his voice was real.

"Well, if I thought you could be trusted, I might let you sleep in the bed with me." Faith couldn't believe she'd uttered the words. She felt Edward turn his head sharply to look at her, but she was overcome with shyness all of a sudden and couldn't make herself look at him.

"Do you mean that?" Disbelief registered in his voice. His breath caught and hung in his lungs at the thought of her trusting him that much. Also at the thought of having to live up to that trust. He really didn't know if he could spend night after night in bed with Faith and not claim her as his own.

Faith couldn't find the strength to make herself repeat her offer.

"Faith? Did you mean what you just said, or did you even say it? Am I just dreading the recliner so badly that I'm hallucinating?"

"I said it," she finally managed to whisper.

"You never cease to amaze me." His voice was low and gruff as he reached over and squeezed Faith's hand.

They were entering Vicksburg's city limits. Again, Faith thrilled at the beauty of the old city. Grand old mansions were reminiscent of a time when the state was one of the wealthiest in the nation. The city perched high on a bluff, overlooking the mighty Mississippi River, and everywhere were reminders of the fierce battle that took place during the Civil War. Edward had promised to take her to see the Vicksburg National Cemetery, where more than 17,000 Union soldiers were buried. He'd explained that the Confederate soldiers were buried in the Vicksburg City Cemetery, and they would go and see that also.

They were getting close to his parent's neighborhood. Edward was turning left at a green light when all of a sudden he made a throaty exclamation. Faith turned in the direction he was looking just in time to see the car bearing down on them, coming straight at her.

She screamed, was aware of a grinding crunch, then nothing.

**She opened her eyes slowly and looked up into Edward's concerned face.**

"Are you okay?" His voice was hoarse with anxiety.

"I have a terrible pain in my back," was all she could say before the world slipped away again.

**Would they never get to the hospital?** Edward was frantic. He looked down at Faith's pale face and held her hand tighter, cursing the slowness of the ambulance that was speeding them toward the closest hospital.

Typically, the drunk who'd hit them had not even been scratched. If he'd been sober enough to know what was going on, Edward would gladly have remedied that. But why beat a man who didn't even know what he'd done?

But now Edward had to concentrate on Faith. She would be okay! He refused to think of the possibility of losing her. Not when he had finally found the only woman in the world he had ever loved.

The ambulance was stopping. They were finally at the hospital.

It seemed to Edward like hours had passed as he paced the floor of the emergency waiting room. Finally, a nurse came into the room.

"I—I'm afraid we couldn't save the baby, Mr. Brenner. I'm sure you were aware that your wife was pregnant? The doctor tried, but just couldn't save it." She was genuinely concerned, but Edward's voice cut her off.

"How's my wife? Is she okay? May I go in to her now?" Agitation made his voice impatient.

"No, Mr. Brenner, you can't go in yet. They're still examining her, but she's going to be all right." The nurse spoke in her most professional, calm voice.

"They're still examining her, but she's going to be all right! Right! That makes a lot of sense. How much longer is it going to take before I can see her?" He was ready to shake the nurse.

"Here, take this, and you'll relax a little." She handed him a pill and a cup of water. "Your wife's going to be fine. She seems to have only gotten some cuts and scratches, and possibly a concussion. Now stop worrying. Just swallow the pill and relax." She left Edward alone in the room.

Edward looked at the pill scornfully before tossing it into the closest wastebasket. He tried to drink the water, but it was warm, so he tossed it in with the pill and sat down to wait.

**As Faith opened her eyes, she was vaguely aware of the white room around her.** Slowly, as her vision cleared, she realized she was in a hospital room and that she was alone. No—she wasn't alone. Someone was clutching her hand.

Gradually and painfully she moved her head until her eyes rested on the figure beside her bed. To her still foggy amazement she realized the figure was Edward. He was on his knees with her hand tightly clutched in both of his and his head rested on the three entwined hands. Was he asleep?

Then, as consciousness came flooding in on Faith, she realized he was crying. Puzzled, she was about to speak when Edward raised a tear-soaked face to look at her.

"Faith!" he exclaimed. He looked older, somehow. And very tired. "Faith? Can you see me?" He half way rose from his kneeling position.

"Of course I can see you. Why wouldn't I be able to see you?" She tried to smile, and wondered why her voice felt and sounded so weak.

Edward took a deep breath and held her hand against his cheek and closed his eyes.

"Edward, what's wrong? Are you sick? Did you get hurt in the wreck? How long has it been since it happened? An hour? Two hours?"

He pressed the button to beckon a nurse before he answered her.

His smile was tender as he recaptured her hand and gently caressed it. "It's been exactly a week, my love."

A nurse stuck her head in the room and asked, "Yes, Mr. Brenner?" Then she saw Faith's open eyes and hurried to the bedside.

"Why, Sugar! You finally woke up!" She began her usual routine of checking Faith's pulse, taking her temperature, and talking all at the same time. "See, Mr. Brenner? We told you she'd come around at any time."

While the nurse puttered around, Faith watched. A week? She looked at Edward, who smiled. His smile and eyes seemed to reach down to Faith's heart and lift it to her throat. Had he truly just now called her his love? Or was that just something her muddled brain had imagined? And why did he look so haggard? Hadn't he gotten any rest while she was unconscious? He must have been extremely worried about Frank's baby, she told herself, as she tried to turn onto her side.

Only then did she realize she couldn't feel her feet and legs. She felt nothing from her hips down.

The nurse finished and started for the door when Edward stopped her. "Aren't you going to call the doctor?"

"He'll be around in about thirty minutes. He can examine Mrs. Brenner then," she answered in her "don't try to tell me when to call the doctor" voice.

"Well, I think he should be called right away," Edward insisted.

"Of course," answered the nurse, slightly perturbed at Edward's attitude.

When the door closed, Edward turned back to Faith. "Whew! I'm glad you're back. You had me worried sick."

Faith tried to move her feet again, and again felt nothing. Maybe they're just asleep, she reasoned. She'd get the feeling back in her legs soon, she was sure.

"Edward, what happened? Were you hurt?"

"No, not a scratch. The other car hit your side, and I just got a few bruises. And the drunk that hit us didn't even get bruised." His voice held scorn for the drunk driver.

"Have you found out anything about the drug dealers?"

"Do you think I could leave this room before I found out if you were okay or not? And besides, Jeff is still on the case. He'll let me know if there are any changes." His eyes held hers tenderly. Something was very different about Edward, Faith decided. But what?

"Well, you should have continued your work. I was in good hands."

"I'll worry about work later. Right now, I need to call Dad and Mother, and let them know that you're awake."

While Edward was on the phone Faith tried to move her legs again, but was disappointed to find she still had no feeling where her legs should be. Suddenly a thought made her weak. Had she lost her legs in the wreck? She managed to raise her body off the bed enough to see her legs and feet. They were there!

She fell back on the pillow weak from relief, now, more than exhaustion. But what was wrong with her legs?

"Why the worried look?" Edward hung the phone on the receiver and turned to Faith. "Your worries are over. Dad and Mom are coming as soon as they can get here, and as soon as the doctor will release you, we'll take you home so you can recover in peace and quiet. Then I can get on with my sleuthing. Does that sound good?"

"It sounds wonderful." She hesitated. "Edward, what's wrong with my legs?"

"Your legs?" There was sudden concern in his voice.

"I can't move them."

"*Whaaat?* You can't move them at all? Are you sure?"

"Positive. I've tried ever since I've been awake, and I can't feel them. I thought at first they were asleep, but it's been long enough for the feeling to come back, if that's all it was. I just can't feel anything! They don't even feel like they're attached to my body. It feels like I don't even have any legs." She was trying hard not to panic.

"I'll get the doctor," Edward said. Turning, he almost ran over the doctor, who was coming in the door.

"Dr. Bradford, Faith says she can't move her legs!" Edward said before the doctor could even speak.

"What? Why, sure you can," he said in a patronizing voice as he moved to her bedside. "You've just been off of them for so long they're out of practice." He picked up one of her legs and moved it back and forth, then up and down.

"Come, Nurse Brown," he said to the young nurse who had followed him into the room. "Let's get Mrs. Brenner on her feet and show her that her legs are okay."

Faith glanced at Edward, who smiled at her encouragingly. She found herself being propelled by skillful hands to the bedside.

"Okay, let's stand up," the doctor instructed, as he and the nurse placed their hands under her arms and lifted her to her feet.

When Faith was on her feet, she had a strange sensation of floating on air. She still couldn't feel anything, and without their help, would have fallen straight to the floor.

"Now, take a few steps. It'll feel odd at first, but you'll soon get back in step." The doctor chuckled at his own joke.

Faith tried to move one of her legs to take a step, but it wouldn't cooperate. She tried the other one, but no response from it either.

"Try to move them, Mrs. Brenner," the doctor encouraged.

"I'm trying, Doctor, but nothing's happening. I feel nothing." Irritation tinged her voice, because she was trying so hard that perspiration had popped out on her forehead.

"Okay, let's get back on the bed." Puzzled, he stood looking down at her.

"Your legs have felt this way ever since you've been awake?"

"Yes. I was going to turn over when I realized I couldn't feel anything from my hips down."

"Approximately how long has she been awake?" the doctor asked, looking at Edward.

"About fifteen minutes," Edward said.

"Then her legs aren't just 'asleep.' Umm. We'd better take some X-rays. Nurse Brown, make preparations, please. We'll take Mrs. Brenner up about ten o'clock. Now, don't worry, Mrs. Brenner, everything is going to be just fine. The X-rays we took right after the wreck show no signs of a broken pelvis or any broken bones, so I'm sure this is just a temporary situation." He patted her hand and left the room.

Faith looked at the closed door, then at Edward. His look was searching, as his eyes met hers. He pulled a chair close beside her bed and took her hand and stroked it gently.

"Faith, I feel responsible for this. If I've messed up your life, I'll never forgive myself." His voice was jagged with concern.

"Oh, that's ridiculous. You didn't cause the wreck. You're as much a victim as I am. You just didn't get hurt as badly. Now don't even think such a thing as that."

"But I should have followed my first instincts and not have gotten you involved in this drug mess in any way, shape or form."

"Edward, you're just tired. You look extremely bushed." She reached out and laid her hand on the rough stubble that covered his cheek.

"Well, I should think he should," spoke his mother from the doorway. "He wouldn't let anybody relieve him up here. I offered to stay, but *no*, nobody could stay with you except him." She looked at her husband, who had come in behind her.

"See, she looks as beautiful as ever. I knew she'd be just fine."

Faith was glad to see Edward's parents. Was it true that Edward wouldn't let anyone stay with her except him? She met his eyes, and if she hadn't known better she would have thought they were filled with love.

He was probably afraid she would talk about the drug ring in her unconscious state, so he didn't want anyone with her but himself, a small voice of reason reminded her.

"How are you, my dear?" Edward's father asked, peering down at her lovingly. She didn't have to question the love of her in-laws. She knew in her heart that they already, in this brief time, loved her dearly. "You've really had us worried," he continued. "Edward, you truly have a lovely wife. She's beautiful even after having gone through such a hard week. But, Son, you look dreadful. Can't you get some rest now?"

"Yes, Edward," interrupted his mother, "you know I'll be only too happy to stay with Faith while you go take a much needed nap."

"Mom, Dad, Faith doesn't seem to have any feeling in her legs. Dr. Bradford has her scheduled for X-rays at ten o'clock. After we get the results from that, then I promise I'll get some rest."

"Can't feel her legs?" the older couple chorused at the same time.

"Don't worry," Faith tried to reassure them. "The doctor doesn't seem to think it's a problem. I'm going to be fine."

"Why, of course," Edward's father said. "With the modern technology they have these days, they can fix just about anything." He seemed to be trying to convince himself as much as anyone else.

After they had visited for a while, Edward's parents left with the promise that they would be back in the afternoon to check on her and relieve Edward of his post.

When they'd gone, Edward went to the window and stood looking out at the clear blue sky. The time he had dreaded so much had come. He couldn't put it off any longer. He had to tell her about the baby. How would she react? Would she be relieved to be rid of a baby she hadn't wanted in the first place? And how would this affect their relationship?

"Edward?" Faith called softly from the bed.

He turned to her, and she could see the distress in his eyes.

"What's wrong, Edward? I've sensed all morning that you have something to tell me. Please tell me what's troubling you."

He sat on the bed beside her and leaned over and kissed her lips softly. His father was right. Even after this week of being sick, she still looked beautiful.

"My love, we lost our baby in the wreck." Tears came to his eyes as he spoke.

A low groan started deep inside Faith and welled up from her throat as tears poured from her eyes. Edward gathered her close and held her tightly against his comforting chest as she cried.

She hadn't realized how accustomed she'd become to thinking about the baby as part of herself until it was gone. She'd started to feel a close bond with the child growing inside her, knowing she would no longer be alone in the world after she gave birth to her baby. But now she would have no one. Now Edward wouldn't need to stay married to her. She'd be alone again.

She cried for her lost baby. She cried for her oncoming loneliness. But most of all she cried because she knew she would lose Edward.

# Chapter 7

**Faith rolled her wheelchair out onto the balcony, where she sat and enjoyed the beautiful spring day.** Two weeks had passed since the day she had gained consciousness into her new world. Two weeks of tests and experiments had revealed no reason for her legs to be without sensation. Five different specialists had been called in to study her case, and none of them could offer a solution. Their closest prognostication was a traumatized nerve in her back. They would watch her for a few weeks and see how things developed.

Faith felt frustrated that no one could give her an answer to her condition. Was it temporary? Or was she facing a life of living in a wheelchair? She was amazed that in the short two-week period she'd already learned how to manipulate herself in and out of the chair to use the bathroom and take a shower. A special chair had been placed in the bathtub so she could sit and bathe herself, then turn the shower head on to rinse off. Her biggest task was getting in and out of the bed. She still had to have help because the bed was so high and it was hard to pull herself up onto it.

Faith's hand went to her stomach as it had done so many times in the past two weeks. She missed that other life she had been so swiftly growing to love. She hadn't realized how much she'd been looking forward to having a baby to love and take care of. Someone who would love her back, unconditionally. Someone to take away the loneliness that had been her constant companion since she lost her parents.

Edward's parents were heartbroken that they had come so close to having a grandchild, only to have it snatched from them before they could even meet it. But Edward had reassured them that there would be another chance.

Why had he made that commitment to them, knowing that now there would be no reason for them to stay married? Sometimes Faith couldn't figure out his motives. She knew he didn't love her and that he would want a divorce as soon as possible now there was no child to give his name to. And yet he almost as good as promised his parents another grandchild. Did he have someone else lined up for marriage as soon as their divorce was final? Maybe Lona? Surely that was it.

Faith turned her face into the ray of sunlight that drifted through the overhanging limbs and let the tears fall freely. She'd lost her baby, she would lose Edward, and she didn't know if she would ever walk again. Her life seemed more desolate than it ever had.

"Here you are." Edward's voice was close behind Faith before she realized he was approaching. Quickly she tried to dry her eyes, but not before he had seen the tears.

"What's wrong, Faith? Are you in pain?" The concern in his voice brought fresh tears to her eyes.

"No," she tried to smile, embarrassed that she'd been caught. "I've just been indulging in a little self-pity."

Edward pulled a chair close to her and sat down. Taking her hand in his, he gently kissed it. "Well, thank goodness."

Her chest ached with the emotions that his closeness and tenderness aroused in her.

"Why do you say that?" Her voice was almost a whisper.

"Because now I know you're human. You've been a real trooper these past two weeks, but I knew you were going to explode if you didn't let it out. Do you feel better now? If not, I've got two strong shoulders you can borrow to cry on." The sparkle in his eyes lightened Faith's mood more than the crying jag she'd just been on. At this moment, the easiest thing in the world would be to go into those strong arms and let him hold her forever, but she knew she must talk to him about the subject she'd just been thinking about.

"Edward, I've been thinking that if there isn't a baby for you to be concerned about giving a name, there's no use for us to continue with this marriage. You can be free again. Free to marry someone you really love. Free to have babies of your own. We can get a divorce as soon as the arrangements can be made to see a lawyer."

Once she'd started the words came quickly, but the expression on Edward's face wasn't what she'd expected. He let go of her hand and stood up. He looked down at her for a long moment before answering.

"Are you really in that much of a hurry to be rid of me? I'm sorry if you are—for more reasons than one, but you're going to have to put up with me for a little longer."

Faith couldn't understand the open sadness in his voice. She thought he'd be excited to be able to get on with his life.

"But why? I see no reason to postpone the inevitable," she reasoned.

"Faith, listen to me. What do you think my family would say if I divorced you now? They'd probably disown me if I divorced my wife just when she needed me the most. And what would my friends think? We've done a good job of making everyone think this marriage was made in heaven, so surely you don't expect me to play the jerk by divorcing you as soon as you get in a wheelchair."

"You mean we must go on with this farce indefinitely?"

"I'm afraid so." It hurt him to hear her speak so coldly about their marriage. He'd hoped that by now she was developing some feelings for him.

"How long?" She felt panic rise in her for a moment. Surely he would soon guess that the love she pretended to have for him was real. She couldn't bear to have him guess her secret. Couldn't bear to see pity in his eyes when he told her he could never share her feelings.

"How long are you going to be in that chair?"

"Oh, Edward! No! That might be for life!"

"Then it'll be for life," he said. At least he'd have time to make her love him.

"No! I won't ruin your life!"

"I don't consider it ruining my life, and besides, I don't know what you can do about it."

"I'll file for divorce myself." Resolution sounded in each word.

He was smiling now, seeming to enjoy her moment of frustration.

"On what grounds?" he asked, the twinkle coming back into his beautiful blue eyes.

"On—on—on cruelty." Faith snatched a word from the air.

"Are you equipped with proof of this alleged cruelty?"

"Mental cruelty can't necessarily be proven. I'll do whatever I have to to get this divorce." Faith's voice was harsh. She loved him too much to allow him to sacrifice his life and future happiness for her.

Misreading the desperation in her voice, Edward's reaction was instant.

"Well, I hadn't dreamed you hated life with me so much. I'll see what I can do about it." And he turned and walked away from her.

It hurt Faith to hear the sarcasm in his voice, and have it directed at her. But if making him angry with her was what it took, then that's the price she'd have to pay. There was no need for his life to be ruined forever just because of a mistake she'd made. The mistake that had led ultimately to the condition she was in. If she had never become pregnant with his brother's child, she wouldn't be in this situation. She only had herself to blame, therefore she would do her suffering alone.

She turned the wheelchair slowly around and made her way to her room. She was almost to the door of their bedroom when a voice behind her made her come to an abrupt halt. She turned to look into the gloating eyes of Lee Silverhill.

"Well, that was an interesting little conversation between you and your husband."

His smile turned Faith's stomach. All she could think of was what a lowlife he was for being involved in drug dealing.

"Are you sure you want that divorce? Life can be awfully lonely when it's spent alone. Especially alone and in a wheelchair. Say, I heard you lost yours and Edward's and Frank's baby. That's too bad, isn't it? Now you don't have a real reason to try to hang on to all the Brenner money."

He was leaning over her with his hands on each arm of the wheelchair. His breath smelled of whisky and cigarettes. Fear made Faith's throat tighten.

"Maybe you'd like to shove me in the pool again? Only you can't now, can you?" His sneer was ugly.

"She can't, but I can. In fact, I can do a lot more than shove your sorry ass in a pool of water." Edward's face matched his voice. Anger made the veins on his forehead stand out.

"I heard the whole conversation, Lee. I waited to see just how far you'd go. You are a cheap, low-life bastard. You'd better get out of here before I do something I've wanted to do to you for a long time. And stay away from my wife! I mean it. Don't come near her again when she's alone."

Lee's face was distorted with rage at being caught in his little intimidation game. He started to respond, but decided not to push his luck. He turned on his heel and stalked down the hall.

Edward pushed Faith into their room.

"Now what?" she asked fearfully.

He shrugged with uncertainty. "I don't think he suspects we're getting close to his operation, and I don't want to drive him away from the house or do anything to make him suspicious. So that means you're going to have to face him for a while longer. I'm sorry. Nothing would make me happier than to ask Dad to get him out of this house."

Faith felt sick. She had a foreboding of trouble. A deep feeling of worry that things were about to explode.

**Later that night, Faith sat watching the small TV Edward had bought to go in their room.** Edward had gone downstairs to get a book to read. She felt tired from the stress of the day.

She looked at the bed. She would love to lie down, but she needed to wait for Edward to help her. The bed was one thing she still had trouble with.

Suddenly determination set in, and she headed the wheelchair toward the bed. She would conquer this problem right now. She wanted to lie down, and there was no need for her to have to wait. She pulled the wheelchair close to the bed and wiggled herself close to the edge of its seat. She reached onto the bed as far as she could, grabbed two hands full of the plush comforter, and slowly started to pull herself into a standing position. So far, so good. Once she got on her feet she could just fall over on the bed, and work herself the rest of the way up.

But suddenly she felt the wheelchair move. She had forgotten to lock the wheels! She was slipping, and couldn't stop herself. She tried in vain to grab a stronger hold on the bed, but only managed to pull the comforter after her. She hit the wheelchair, knocking it sideways, and landed on the floor, partly covered with the spread.

She lay still for a moment, barely breathing. Had she broken any bones? She didn't feel any pain, so she must be okay.

She tried to sit up, but one arm was under the wheelchair in a twisted position and she couldn't get it out. The other arm was tangled in the comforter and was under the bed. She was impatiently trying to unwrap her hand from the comforter when she heard the door opening.

She heard Edward's quickly indrawn breath, then he was kneeling beside her.

"Faith! What on earth?" He pushed the wheelchair out of the way. "Are you okay? Are you hurt?"

"No. I'm okay, really." Faith tried to reassure him, embarrassed that he had found her like this. She'd wanted to be on the bed when he returned. She needed to prove to him as much as to herself that she could live without him.

"Come on, then. Let's get you up from the floor." He untangled her arm and stood up. Placing his strong hands under her arms, he lifted her so she could sit on the side of the bed.

She lay back on the pillows and Edward gently lifted her legs onto the bed and covered her with the sheet.

"Well? How did this happen?"

Faith knew she would have to tell him everything. He wouldn't leave it alone until she did.

"I just fell," she answered, not volunteering anything.

"I know you fell. How did you fall? Why did you fall?" She refused to look at him until he took her chin in his hand and turned her face to him.

"I was trying to get on the bed," she answered, looking everywhere except his eyes.

"I thought we'd established that you couldn't get on the bed alone because it was too high."

"But I wanted to do it by myself. I've got to learn to do these things by myself, while I do have someone to pick me up when I fall." She fought the frustrated tears that threatened to surface.

"Are you going somewhere?"

"Edward, you know what I mean." This wasn't helping the stress headache she could feel starting. Why couldn't he just accept what she was trying to do?

"Yes, I know. You're planning to get a divorce, and then what?"

"I'll go back to my own home."

"Who'll be with you to take care of you?"

"I'll take care of myself! I don't need someone with me constantly. There are thousands of people who are in wheelchairs and they live alone and take care of themselves. Why should I be any different than them?"

Edward sat down on the edge of the bed and took her hand in his. "No." His eyes held hers in a determined lock.

"Yes, Edward, I will. I *must.* Can't you see this is something I must do?" Desperation sounded in her voice.

"But why? Why can't you just let me take care of you?" He didn't think he'd ever seen anyone as self-willed and stubborn as this woman before him.

"You know why. I refuse to live a life of deceitfulness, like we're living, for myself. I would have done it for the baby, but not for myself. And, besides that, you have your life to live. Please try to understand."

"I'm trying to understand. But you spend a lot of time worrying about my life. I'm quite old enough to take care of myself, Faith."

"Maybe I feel the same way. Have you ever thought of that?"

"No, I haven't." Resignation and sadness sounded in Edward's deep voice. "If you're determined to have this divorce, I'll make arrangements for someone to come in and check on you every day, after the divorce is final."

"Edward—"

"No! No arguing. Either you compromise and let me provide someone to help you, or you don't get the divorce." Finality sounded in his voice.

"You are a hard man to try to reason with," Faith said. She finally had the answer she'd been trying to get from him, and she was totally depressed.

Edward slowly raised her hand to his lips and kissed each finger, one at a time. "But I can be really easy to get along with if I'm given half a chance. Why don't you stop being in such a hurry for this divorce and find out just how much fun I can be."

The teasing note in his voice made Faith's blood run hot. She felt the color flood her face. If he only knew just how much she wanted to do what he suggested, he wouldn't tease her about it so freely.

"Did Lee stay for the night?" she asked, trying to change the subject.

Edward's laughter filled the room. Suddenly he felt jubilant. Yes, he'd give her a divorce, but only after he'd exhausted all his efforts to win her love. Caution was over. He was going to charm her if it took the rest of his life. "Why are you trying to change the subject? Don't you think I might possibly be able to curb my stubbornness and be fun to live with?"

"You might if you found someone who could put up with you." Faith wished the conversation would come to an end before she broke down and confessed how she really felt.

"Well, you're my legal wife. I think I'll show you how nice and lovable I can really be." He lay down beside her and put his arm around her midriff. He was lowering his mouth to hers when he became aware of the astonished look on her face.

He drew back quickly and said, "Baby, I'm sorry, I didn't mean to scare you."

"No, no, you didn't scare me."

"Then why that look on your face?"

Faith smiled at him as she reached up and put her fingertips on his lips.

"I think I'm getting the feeling back in my legs."

"Faith, are you sure? How can you tell?"

"My legs are tingling like they have a million needles in them."

"Do you want to try to stand up?" Edward raised himself from the bed.

"Yes," she answered, sitting up on the bed.

Edward slid his hands under her arms and slowly raised her to her feet. She could actually feel her feet under her again! Her joy would have been complete except for the excruciating pain that was shooting though both legs, causing her to sit back down on the side of the bed.

Edward knelt beside her. "What? Talk to me. What are you feeling?"

"I have a lot of pain in my legs, but it seems to be easing up a little now."

"I'd better call the doctor." He started to stand, but Faith's hand on his shoulder stopped him.

"Edward, calm down for a moment and let's see what's happening here," she admonished. "Remember how your legs felt when you were a kid and had them tucked up under you, or were sitting on something with your legs hanging down, then you tried to stand on them? That's exactly how my legs feel now."

"Why don't you lie back down and let me exercise them a little and see if that helps."

Faith did as he suggested, lying back on the bed. Edward took one leg at a time and slowly worked them up and down and back and forth, repeatedly, for several minutes. He massaged her legs from just above her knees to her ankles. Soon the pain started to subside.

Finally, Faith stopped him. "They feel better. Let me try to stand again."

Edward helped her to her feet. Keeping an arm around her, he said, "Try to take a step."

Faith tried. Her legs felt better, but they still hurt a little. She loosened her grip on Edward's hand and stood alone. Tears filled her eyes. How wonderful just to be able to stand without help.

Taking her cue, Edward backed away from her only the slightest. He held out his arms and motioned for her to take a step toward him. Cautiously, she took a step, stopped, and then took another. With each step toward him, Edward backed up one. They did that in a small circle, with Edward leading her back to the side of the bed.

When he felt the bed behind him, he stopped. But Faith, intent on each step, wasn't paying attention and walked right into him. His arms closed around her and pulled her close.

"You're going to be okay. I was so worried that I had caused you to spend your life in a wheelchair. But you're going to be okay, now." His lips covered hers in a kiss so tender that it made Faith's already weak legs even weaker, and she could feel them buckling under her.

Edward lowered her to the bed and sat down beside her. Faith looked into his eyes. So that was it. He felt he'd caused her to be in this situation because he'd been driving when the drunk ran into them. That's why he'd been so determined to take care of her. He thought it was all his fault.

But why did he keep kissing her when there was no one around to try to impress? Maybe he really did care for her. Maybe—

"No." She headed her thoughts off before they could go any further, but didn't realize she'd spoken aloud until Edward looked at her with raised eyebrows.

"'No' what, baby? What are you saying 'no' to now? I haven't said anything, and I don't think you were reading my mind because your face isn't red enough."

Frantically searching her mind for a reason for having blurted out the word, Faith said lamely, "I was just thinking that you still think you caused the wreck, and I was saying 'no' that you didn't." She hoped her answer would satisfy him, and apparently it did, because he changed the subject.

"I guess we'd better keep this just between you and me for a few more days. We'll practice walking in the mornings before I leave for work and at night. Don't walk if I'm not here. And don't do anything differently than you've been doing. You might get caught, and then our cover will be blown. I hate to keep this wonderful news from Dad and Mom, but if Lee finds out the truth, he'll surely get suspicious as to why we're still here. I'll call the doctor from work tomorrow. I'm sure he'll want to see you."

**The next day, Faith sat on the balcony and looked at the scene below.** Her thoughts were far from the things her eyes were focused on.

She was remembering earlier this morning, when Edward had gently shaken her awake. She had been dreaming, and was surprised to look up into his blue eyes. For a moment she couldn't bring her mind to focus on where she was. Then, realizing, she'd smiled a slow, lazy smile.

"Well, I'm glad to see you smile. I thought for a moment you were going to slug me for disturbing your sleep."

"I ought to, but this day, I want to wake up and walk, walk, walk!" She had sat up and swung her feet to the floor, and stood.

Edward had stayed close by, but offered no help. She took a hesitant step, then another, and then had walked around the room and come back to Edward, her eyes shining with joy. Suddenly, the thrill, the pure exhilaration of being able to walk again had overcome her, and she had thrown her arms around Edward's neck and his arms had tightly engulfed her. For a moment they had shared the joy together before she became aware of their intimate position. She stepped back and looked into Edward's eyes.

"I'm so glad I won't be a burden to you anymore. I hated the thought of you feeling obligated to take care of me for the rest of my life."

"But that's what I promised to do in our wedding vows, remember?" His answer was so honest, Faith's heart jumped to her throat.

"But those weren't real vows, we both know that." Her voice was almost a whisper.

"Weren't they? They seemed real to me. 'To love, cherish, and protect, for better or worse, until death do us part'." Very slowly, he took her into his arms, and very slowly, very gently he kissed her. Exploring, savoring, glorying in her soft, willing mouth.

Then he eased her down into the waiting wheelchair, and leaning over her, again brushed her lips with his.

"I'll see you later. Don't take any chances while I'm gone."

Faith still felt flushed and excited from the incident. It was becoming harder and harder to figure him out. Why did he say those things if he didn't mean them? Didn't he realize she could take them seriously? Were they serious?

No! No! NO! She *had* to stop thinking like that. She just wanted him to love her so badly she was starting to believe it. Maybe she'd even imagined he'd said those things to her about the wedding vows. She knew he'd never have chosen her under different circumstances, the old doubts reminded her.

She had to get out of this house. She had to give Edward his freedom, so she could get on with her life and not keep tormenting herself like she was doing. She'd just call a lawyer and get the ball rolling, so when Edward did get to the bottom of this case they wouldn't have to wait so long to get the divorce.

The Yellow Pages seemed to be the logical place to look for a lawyer since she didn't know any, and on impulse, she wheeled herself back to the room. She thumbed through the phone book until she found a name that appealed to her. She reached for the receiver and started to dial the number, when an arm reached around her and hung the receiver up.

"Oh, no, you don't. Not yet." Edward's voice was close as he wheeled the chair around to face him.

Faith didn't volunteer any explanation. She didn't know what to say.

Edward sat down on the bed facing her. His face was somber, and his eyes had lost their usual twinkle.

"My, my. You sure seem anxious to get this marriage over with. Could you possibly stand my company until I clear up this case? Am I asking too much?" His voice was low, and Faith knew she was imagining it, but it seemed there was a sadness laced through his words. She reached over and laid her palm on his face.

"Oh, Edward, I just wanted to ask some questions. I'll make a deal with you. If you promise to tell me when this case is settled to your satisfaction, then I won't mention divorce again until you say so."

"That's a deal I'll shake on." Relief sounded in his voice as he held out his hand. Faith laid her hand in his, but instead of shaking hands as he'd offered, he brought her hand up to his lips and kissed it.

"Why are you back?" she asked, trying to hide the excitement he always caused to flood through her. "You just left a little while ago."

"There's not a lot going on at the office today, and I just couldn't get you out of my mind, so I decided to come back and see if you wanted to go joy riding."

"Somewhere I can walk around?" Excitement flooded in her voice.

"That was the general idea," Edward said, loving the anticipation on her face. Why couldn't she see how lovely she was? She had the kind of face that mirrored her every emotion, and he was certain he'd seen love in her eyes when she looked at him. He had to hold on to that hope right now.

"I called the doctor this morning, and he said he's not surprised you're regaining the feeling in your legs. He said to encourage you to get all the exercise you can, and he wants to see you in a week."

"Okay, but when are we going for that ride?" She was impatient to get out of the wheelchair and walk.

"Right now," Edward said, and guided her wheelchair down the stairs to the car.

After they were settled in the car, Edward said, "I thought we'd grab a bite of lunch, then head out to the Military Park. There are some places in the park that you can walk around and nobody can see you. We have to be careful, just in case we bump into someone who knows us."

"I don't care where it is, just as long as I can walk around and feel my legs under me."

"I know of this really quaint little place that I want to take you for lunch. It's in a neighborhood that's kind of questionable, but the cooking is straight down-home southern style, and is wonderful. A lot of business types go there for lunch, because most working people just don't cook and eat like that anymore. It'll be crowded, but it's worth it. Is that okay with you?"

"Sure," Faith agreed. She didn't care what or where she ate as long as she was with Edward, and as long as she could walk.

Soon Edward pulled the car up in front of a small brick building that looked like it had been built in the 1940s. An unusually tall sign standing beside the building seemed to scream the name "SMILEY'S."

When Edward stopped the car Faith reached for her door handle, but Edward's hand stopped her.

"You'd best use the chair here. There might be someone who knows me. I come here often when I'm in Vicksburg, so I'll probably run into someone who'll recognize me."

When Edward pushed Faith through the restaurant door, Faith was dismayed to see how small the place was. It was just one room that had tables and chairs pushed so close to each other there was hardly room to walk past, much less get a wheelchair through. But

Edward found a vacant spot and managed to get Faith's wheelchair pushed up to a table where several other people were sitting.

"Are these places taken?" he asked.

"No, feel free to join us," came the friendly answer from several people at once.

"I'll go order for us. I'll be right back." And he left her sitting there with strangers while he went up to the buffet style food display and told the serving ladies what he wanted.

He came back with two plates loaded with turnip greens, chicken and dumplings, cornbread, and apple pie. Making a second trip, he brought back two large glasses of iced tea.

Faith was impressed at how good the food was. She enjoyed every bite, but most of all enjoyed just sitting and sharing small talk with Edward.

Even though the food was delicious, she was relieved when they finally left and headed for the park. She wasn't prepared for the sensations that came over her when they entered Vicksburg National Military Park, with all the white tombstones lined up in perfect rows. They seemed so cold and informal. Looking around at the cannons, mounted guns and other signs of the war, Faith felt a heaviness of heart for all the lives that had been lost here, for all the lives that were forever changed as a result of a country divided against itself.

She was relieved when Edward stopped the car in a secluded spot where they couldn't be seen by anyone except an occasional tourist strolling by.

"Okay. Now you can get out and stretch your legs."

They walked for about fifteen minutes before Edward stopped on a grassy knoll. "Let's rest here for a few minutes," he suggested. "You haven't walked in a while, and you're going to have some sore muscles tomorrow, so let's don't overdo it." They sat down and leaned against a huge old monument that protected them from any watchful eyes.

As they soaked up the sun, Edward told Faith about his ancestors and their role in the Civil War. She was amazed at his knowledge of his ancestors. It made her wish she knew more about her own.

"And what about you, Faith? Where are your ancestors from?" As he asked the questions he shifted position and lay down on his back, resting his head in her lap and gazing up into her eyes.

Too astonished for words, Faith just sat and stared down at his upturned face.

A wide grin spread across his face, but he acted as if this were an everyday action on his part. "Well? Where are they from?" he insisted.

"My mom was mostly English," Faith started hesitantly, still wondering how to respond to Edward's warm head pressing against her thighs.

"Mmmm, this is even softer than it looked," Edward interrupted her, as he nestled his head deeper into her lap.

Faith could feel heat mounting in her face. If Edward noticed, hopefully he'd think it was from walking too long.

"Yes? Go on. Your mother was mostly English. And your dad?"

"My dad was mostly French. But I don't know a lot about my lineage. Listening to you talk makes me want to know more about mine."

"Well, we can just look into it. We'll call or write the Mormon Church in Salt Lake City, Utah, and they'll help us with information."

"Do you know how to fix everything?" she asked, glancing down at him.

"What do you mean?"

Without realizing it, Faith had started softly stroking the top of Edward's head. His hair was thick and soft, and she loved running her fingers through it.

"You just seem to know how to solve all my problems. You know so much about everything that I feel protected from the real world when I'm with you." She realized she'd said too much as soon as the words left her mouth. This beautiful day and the sad surroundings were putting her in a philosophical state of mind.

"Then why are you in such a hurry to leave me?" Edward's voice was serious as he looked up into her eyes.

"I'm only in a hurry to leave you for your own good," she answered, still sifting her fingers through his hair.

Why couldn't this moment last forever, she wondered, as she gazed down into the blue eyes that had become so dear to her. She could feel herself being drawn, as if some magnetic force were pulling her, and she lowered her head and placed her lips on his in a timid, exploring kiss. But when she tried to raise her lips from his, he placed his strong hand at the back of her lowered head and pressed her lips even closer as he devoured her mouth.

Edward released her mouth just long enough to rise to a sitting position, facing her. She was pinned against the monument and he trapped her lips again in a kiss that was different than any she'd ever experienced. His tongue plunged deeply into her mouth, and the sensation that ripped through Faith's body shook her to her very soul. She felt as if she'd been claimed and branded.

His mouth left hers and trailed down her neck, on down to the gentle swell of her breasts. He cupped each side of her breasts and pushed them together to make the cleavage deeper, then inserted his tongue into the cleavage and licked back and forth, driving Faith out of her mind with desire.

"Edward, please—you have to stop." Had she actually said the words out loud, or just thought them?

"Why, Faith?" His voice was hoarse with desire. "Why do I have to stop?"

"Because if you don't, I won't be able to," she admitted, her voice barely more than a whisper.

"That's what I wanted to hear, baby. That and much more, but that's enough for right now. Look what you do to me," he said, and took her hand and placed it on his bulging crotch.

Faith's eyes grew large as her hand came into contact with the swollen area of Edward's body.

"I do that to you?" Disbelief sounded in her voice.

"Yes, baby. You do that to me more times than you ever know."

Their eyes held for a moment, then Edward gently kissed her again.

"We'd better get back to the house. Mom and Dad will be back and wondering where we are. But, Faith, we will continue this conversation later," he promised.

His voice was sincere, and Faith knew he meant it. He wasn't just kidding with her this time. A charge of expectant electricity shot through her body.

# Chapter 8

**With the help of one of his two shady-looking companions, Lee Silverhill roughly shoved Faith into the back of a utility van parked outside the Brenners' house.**

"Leave the wheelchair just like it is. That way the first one home will know something's happened to her," Lee snarled to his goons.

Faith caught a glimpse of the overturned chair before the side door of the van was slammed shut. There were no seats in the back of the van, and she lay sprawled on the floor where she'd landed when she was roughly pushed into the vehicle. Using only her arms and upper body, so as not to arouse any suspicions that she could use her legs, she pulled herself into a sitting position and leaned against the wall of the van.

Lee had brought along two men to help him do his dirty work. Probably the same two that were with him when she had seen him in the barn.

All three crowded into the front seat of the van. Lee had the vehicle in motion before the passenger door was even closed. He squealed the tires as he pulled onto the highway, speeding away from the Brenner house.

"Where are you taking me?" Faith asked, after the van had leveled out and Lee seemed to have more control of it.

"You keep your trouble-making mouth shut back there, and just possibly, you might live to see another day. I'm not sure how many more, but maybe at least one more." He snickered knowingly and elbowed the guy beside him. As if on cue all three men laughed loudly, causing Faith to imagine her doom was already cast.

She sat in silence and tried to calm her racing pulse. This was *not* a good situation. She didn't really think Lee would kill her, but how could she be sure? She didn't know anything about him. And if he took the same drugs he was selling, he might be capable of doing anything. Look what Frank had done to her. She had to keep her head and come up with a plan to escape.

She was sitting on the floor of the van, so she was unable to see out the windows to tell which direction they were going. She decided to just watch the treetops and listen for sounds. Maybe she'd be able to see something she recognized.

They hadn't gone far when Lee turned onto a side street. Faith could hear children laughing and shouting, so she knew they were in a neighborhood. But where? Where was he taking her? Lee slowed the van, and Faith thought he was stopping until he yelled, "You kids get outa the way! Can't you see this van?" He blared the horn angrily.

"Man, I don't mean to tell you what to do, but you don't need to draw attention to us." It was the first time either of the other two men had spoken, and Faith could tell he was half afraid to say anything.

"You're right," Lee confirmed, "but them damn kids just get on my nerves."

"Yeah, I know." The other man seemed relieved that he'd gotten away with his suggestion.

"But, Mac," Faith was astonished at the cold fury in Lee's quiet voice, "I don't need instructions from you. Remember that in the future."

"Okay," was all the response that was offered, but Faith heard the fear in that one word.

Suddenly she felt the hair stand up on the back of her neck, and she, too, knew fear. What kind of man was Lee Silverhill? *Could* he kill her? She knew she'd made a real enemy out of him when she pushed him into the pool at the Brenners' party, but how badly did he really hate her?

Now she understood why Edward had been so afraid for her to become involved in this investigation. Did he know more about Lee than he'd told her?

"Damn these kids!" Lee said again, almost coming to a complete stop to avoid running over several who were playing football in the street.

That's when Faith saw the sign outside her window. High in the air stood the sign that said "SMILEY'S." New hope surged through her. She had a general idea of where she was. Now if they didn't go much further—

She felt the van turn onto another street and proceed at a slower speed. She could see what appeared to be the roofs of tall metal buildings on each side, and sensed they were going into an industrial section. Soon the van eased to a stop.

The three men jumped out, and Faith heard what sounded like a metal door being slid open just as Lee and Mac threw open the van door and reached for her.

She was half carried, half dragged into a huge metal warehouse, and shoved onto a long, flat trailer hooked to a tow motor.

"Jimmy, shut the damn door and come on!" Lee yelled as he jumped on the tow motor and cranked it. Lee already had the tow motor in motion as Jimmy closed the warehouse door and ran to jump on the trailer.

The warehouse was huge, but finally Lee pulled up in front of some offices that were behind a screened barrier. Jimmy hurried to open the door allowing entrance into the office area, while Lee and Mac grabbed Faith under each arm and hauled her off the trailer.

She made sure her legs were limp and dragging behind her. They must not know she could walk until the crucial moment when she could see her way to escape. She tried to stay alert to everything around her. She would find a way out of this, she kept assuring herself.

The two men deposited Faith in the first chair they came to. She looked around at the setting. It looked like it had been a very busy place, at one time. Three desks and chairs sat just inside the screened wall. There were two doors that apparently led into larger offices. A phone was on the desk farthest from Faith. She was sure it didn't still work. The only light in the place was what filtered in through the windows at the top of the building.

Just as she was dreading nightfall and the darkness that would engulf the old building, a bright light flashed on above her head.

"Finally!" Lee barked at smiling Mac, who came out of one of the offices.

"Well, it took me a little bit to find the switch box. But I knew Uncle Rob keeps the electricity turned on in this place, because he has parties here occasionally." He was obviously proud of himself for a job well done.

"Okay, I guess our next move is to call cousin Edward. I think he needs to know his little woman is in danger. Maybe now he'll agree to call off his dogs and get his nose out of my business. Whatcha think, honey? You ain't so high and mighty now, are you? No pools to shove cousin Lee in, right?"

As he talked, his old anger resurfaced, and he walked over to Faith and slapped her across the face. The blow almost knocked her from the chair.

"Oh, I shouldn't have done that, should I?" He reached over and placed his hand gently on the cheek he had just slapped.

"Before this is over, I think I'll just see if cousin Frank was right about how hot you are. He just couldn't say enough about you. I really think he wanted to come back and get some more, but he was sure you'd want him to take care of the bastard kid. You lost it in the wreck, didn't you? That's a shame. It would be kind of nice to see a little Frank running around." As he talked he rubbed Faith's lips with his thumb. As he warmed up to his subject, he placed more pressure on her lips, and just at the right time, she opened her mouth and caught his thumb between her teeth and bit down as hard as she could.

"You bitch!" he yelped, snatching his thumb free. "I'll kill you right now!" He grabbed her throat in both his hands.

"Lee! Lee!" Both of his companions were screaming at him and pulling him off of Faith. "If you kill her, she won't be any good to us."

Reality finally seeped back into Lee's fury-filled senses, and he loosened his grip on Faith's throat.

"You'll pay for this. And it ain't gonna be pretty," he promised, as he turned and walked to the desk with the phone.

Faith watched as he dialed a number and started to talk into the receiver. So the phone worked! If she could only find a way to get to it and call Edward.

She watched as Lee talked. She couldn't hear what he was saying, but he kept looking in her direction. Was he talking about her? Finally, he hung up and walked back to her.

"Now we got cousin Edward's attention! After he makes a few key phone calls to his buddies who are on my trail, he's going to call back and reassure me that my little meeting can go down tonight without any glitches. If you're a good girl, I may even let you talk to him for one last time." The snarl on his face made Faith believe that he could kill her, and would really enjoy doing it, when the time came.

He and his two whipped-puppy companions disappeared into one of the offices. Probably to go over their plans.

What if he did let her talk to Edward? How could she give him a clue as to where she was? Edward knew where SMILEY'S was, but did he know where the warehouses were? Surely he'd be familiar with all the area if he went to SMILEY'S as much as he indicated. She *had* to come up with something.

Would she ever see Edward again? She wished now she had told him just once that she loved him. She smiled softly at the memory of how he'd taught her to take a compliment. She could hear him saying, "Just smile and say thank you." She loved the way he drawled out the word "smi-i-i-ile."

*That's it!* That's how she could let him know where she was. She had a plan. Lee *had* to let her talk with Edward. But she couldn't seem too eager. She had to stay calm.

It seemed like an eternity before the phone rang. Lee and his buddies broke through the office door and headed for the phone across the room. It must be the only phone in the place, she observed.

"Is it a deal?" Lee spoke loudly into the phone. "No, you'll talk to her when I'm convinced you've called off your hit men." He listened for a moment, and then sullenly agreed to something.

"Mac, Jimmy, y'all slide the bitch's chair over here so lover boy can hear her voice."

Faith's heart was pounding loudly in her ears. This would be her only chance. She hoped Edward would pick up on her clues, but she knew she'd only have a few seconds to convey her message.

Lee jammed the receiver into her hand, and Faith stared at him while she raised it to her ear. "Edward, I'm okay," she started before he had a chance to say anything. "I just want to thank you for teaching me to smi-i-i-ile and say thank you, no matter what I wear in the house." She could see Lee reaching for the phone, so she quickly added, "Remember Smiley's—" but Lee jerked the phone from her hand and said into the receiver, "See, she's okay. Now I promise you, if you do exactly like I told you, she'll be back in your bed in no time." And he hung the phone up.

"She'll be dead, but she'll be back in your bed," he added, while his companions laughed and high-fived each other. "And what kind of garbage was that you were saying on the phone?" he asked as an afterthought.

"You wouldn't understand," mumbled Faith, hanging her head in what she hoped looked like great despair.

**As Edward hung up the phone, his entire body was weak with relief that Faith was okay.** But what was she trying to tell him? He knew she was sending him a message, but what? "Smile and say thank you, no matter what I wear in the house?" They'd never talked about what she wore in the house. He scratched his head as he paced the floor. And, "remember Smiley's"? What did that mean? They'd eaten at SMILEY'S, but they hadn't even talked about this case. 'No matter what I wear in the house.' 'Remember Smiley's.' What did she mean? 'Wear in the house.'—'Smiley's'—

*SMILEY'S! Warehouse! That's where she is! In those old warehouses behind SMILEY'S!* Edward called his office to round up everybody to meet him at the warehouses.

**Faith watched as Lee manipulated Mac and Jimmy.** They didn't seem able to think on their own. She wondered where they'd be if they'd never met Lee Silverhill. Maybe their lives would have taken a much better turn.

"Mac," Lee interrupted her thoughts, "why don't you go get something for supper. Just go get some hamburgers and beer. It's going to be a long time until midnight."

When Mac didn't leave instantly, Lee looked at him with a raised eyebrow, "Well? Whatcha waitin' on?"

"I ain't got no money, Lee," Mac said apologetically.

Lee took a twenty-dollar bill out of his wallet and threw it at the man. He grabbed for it, but missed and had to bend and pick it up from the floor.

"Loser," Lee smirked, as Mac left.

Mac soon returned with a sack full of hamburgers and two six-packs of beer. The men tore into the food as if they hadn't eaten in a month.

"What about her?" Jimmy asked.

"She don't need any food," Lee responded. "She could stand to lose some weight, anyway."

"But, Lee—" Jimmy tried to persist, and Faith sent him a silent thank you.

"Shut up and eat, Jimmy, or you won't get any either," Lee snapped, before chugging half a beer.

This was surely a different Lee Silverhill than the Brenners knew. When he was in their home, he was as much a part of their society as they were, but here, he was just another thug.

Faith watched as one six-pack, then the other, disappeared. Maybe they'd be too drunk to have their "meeting" tonight.

Finally Lee, looking tired and sleepy, reached in his pocket and pulled out a revolver and laid it on the table. "Damn thing's hurtin' my ribs," he mumbled, and leaned back in his chair, crossing his arms across his chest and letting his head fall forward.

New hope surged through Faith. If they would all doze off, she'd try to get the gun.

She sat patiently and waited. Just when she'd think they were all asleep, one of them would mumble or squirm, and half rouse the other two.

At one point Lee raised up and said to Faith, "Look, if we all go to sleep, don't let us sleep past 11:30, okay? Now, if you do, and I wake up and I've missed my meeting, I won't have any more use for you. See that gun? I'll blow your brains right out of your head if you let us oversleep. Understand?"

At Faith's quick nod of understanding, he settled back down. Soon all three of them were breathing deeply.

If she were going to find the nerve to do it, now was the time. She had to make herself move. She had sat in the chair, in the same spot, for so long that she wasn't even sure she could get up. But very slowly, afraid to even breathe, she raised herself to a standing position. She moved one foot, then the other. She was about to take another step when Mac let out a big snore. Faith sat quickly back down in the chair.

By now, all three of the men were half awake. "Lee, you just gonna leave that gun laying there while we sleep? What if she gets it?"

"Mac, have you lost your mind? She can't walk, remember? Even if she could walk, she ain't got the guts to try to get my gun with me this close to it. And besides that, I'm a light sleeper. Now the next person that disturbs me before 11:30 is gonna be in a heap of trouble." Again, he kicked back to try to sleep.

Faith sat and waited. After they were all breathing deeply again, she decided to make her move. This time she decided not to be so slow and careful. She stood up and walked quietly to the table and reached for the gun.

When her fingers closed around the cold metal, she wondered if she'd have the nerve to go through with this. She had a gun back home. It was registered, and she'd gone to a firing range many times, so she knew how to use a gun, but firing at a paper target was a lot different than firing at a human being.

She eased the gun off the table and quickly made her way back to her chair.

She picked the chair up and moved it a little further away from the sleeping trio. Somehow that made her more comfortable. Then she sat back down to try to decide on her next move. She couldn't allow Lee to know she could walk until the right time.

Faith glanced at her watch. 10:00. Where was Edward? Had he figured out what she was trying to say to him? She couldn't wait around and find out. She had to act on her own. She could try to get out of the warehouse before the guys woke up, but she'd heard the door squeaking when Jimmy went for supper, and she knew that would wake them up. She could try to get to the phone, but she was sure if she dialed out the noise would wake at least one of them.

The decision was made for her when Lee suddenly opened his eyes and looked straight at her, as if he knew what she was planning.

His eyes went from her to the table where his gun should have been, then back to her and found himself staring down the barrel of his own gun.

"What the hell?" He started to stand up.

"Stay right where you are," Faith commanded in a voice that didn't give room for argument.

"What is it, Lee?" Mac was peering at them through sleep-squinted eyes.

"Somehow the bitch has the gun. Did one of you give it to her? She can't walk, so how did she get it?" By now, he was screaming at his companions.

Faith stood up and leveled the gun more fully at Lee.

"Lee, calm down. Actually, I *can* walk. Don't worry, your puppies are still eating out of your hands." She was amazed at the calm that had settled over her.

He tried a new line of reasoning. "Oh, hell, you can't shoot that gun. You better just give it to me before you hurt yourself."

"Yes, Lee, I can shoot the gun," Faith assured him. She pointed the gun at the half-full can of beer sitting on the table in front of him, and pulled the trigger. The can flew spinning into the air and spewed beer all over the astonished Lee Silverhill.

"You boys line up over there against the wall, and sit down on the floor. *Now!"* she insisted, as Lee started to protest again. Faith shot another can just to prove to them the first time hadn't been an accident.

"Damn! She's good!" Jimmy muttered in admiration.

"You shut the hell up," Lee shouted at him.

"No, *you* shut the hell up, and get over there and *sit down* like I told you to do," Faith commanded. She couldn't believe how calm she felt. She'd probably fall apart any minute.

As the three men lined up and sat down on the floor like obedient schoolchildren, Faith went to the phone. She'd see if she could locate Edward.

**Edward came to a sudden halt.** "Was that a gunshot?" he asked Jeff. They were at the old warehouses, but didn't have a clue as to where to start looking for Faith.

Just then another shot rang out.

"Over here, guys," he called to the police force that had arrived to back them up.

It didn't take them long to find the van parked in front of the warehouse where Faith and her kidnappers were.

Faith was trying to dial the phone and hold the gun on the men when she looked up into the eyes of Edward, who was quietly making his way around the outside of the wire cage.

When he saw Faith holding the gun on the men and dialing the phone, he let out a loud whoop, and then called, "Come on in, men, seems like the situation is under control."

Suddenly the place was filled with policemen cuffing Lee and his goons and reading them their rights.

Edward came to her and gently took the gun from her hand. Only then did she realize how frightened she'd been. She crumpled against Edward's chest and burst into tears.

"It's okay, baby. You're okay, now. Take it easy." As he talked, he stroked her hair. "It's over, Faith. It's finally over."

Slowly her tears subsided as Edward's words sank in. Over. It was all over.

The thought only made her feel worse.

# Chapter 9

**Faith stood on the balcony of the Brenners' home and looked gloomily at the stars above her, without actually seeing them.** Edward was still at the station, finalizing the arrests of Lee and his companions. It would be hours before he returned home.

Then what? What would they say to each other? "Well, it's over, see ya?" Or would they politely shake hands and walk away from each other, like in some movie with a really horrible ending?

Suddenly she knew she couldn't stand the thought of facing Edward. Not now. Not like this. She hurried into her room, took pen and paper off the night stand, and wrote:

> *Edward, I promised I wouldn't mention the divorce again until you did. When you're ready to talk about it, you know where to find me. I'm going home to Texas. I can't take this any longer.*
>
> *Faith*

She quickly threw what clothes she could into one suitcase, called a cab, and went down the back steps of the balcony to wait for the cab to arrive. She didn't want the honking horn to alert the Brenners of what she was doing.

She hated to just walk away from them without saying good-bye, but she'd write them a nice, long letter, telling them how much she'd come to love them.

**Soon she was on a bus headed west.** She rested her head on the back of the seat, wondering briefly whose head had been there before hers. She hoped it had been a clean one.

Her mind wandered back over the past few months. Would she be able to get her old job back? She liked the job, but she had left on such short notice she wouldn't blame her former boss if he refused to take her back. But life would go on. Edward would soon forget her. He'd get on with his life.

Would he remarry soon? The thought of him with someone else tore at her heart.

She still felt saddened at the loss of the baby. Even though, for some strange reason, she continued to have the sensation of the baby's tiny fluttering inside her. Probably just nerves from staying so upset all the time.

She dozed fitfully for a while, then finally drifted into a restless sleep and didn't wake up again until the bus pulled up at the station in her hometown.

She called a cab. Just as the sun was coming up, she pulled up in front of the house that had, at one time, been home to her.

As she entered the house, things that used to be so familiar now seemed strange. She remembered one of her mother's old sayings, "home is where the heart is," and knew her heart surely wasn't here. She'd left it in Mississippi.

She lay down in her old familiar bed and tried to rest, only to find she couldn't go to sleep for the images of Edward swirling through her mind. What had he thought when he got home last night and found her note? Was he furious? Or relieved? Finally in desperation she got out of bed and made a pot of coffee.

She waited until nine a.m., then called her friend, Jan, and asked if she wanted to meet for lunch.

**As the two friends saw each other, they squealed and ran into each other's arms.** After sitting at a table in the restaurant, Jan looked at Faith closely. "Faith, you're looking great. A little sad in the eyes, but great."

Without even thinking, Faith smiled at Jan and said, "Thank you."

Jan clamped her hand over her heart in a feigned heart attack.

Laughing, Faith asked, "What's wrong with you?"

"*You*," her friend answered. "You didn't argue with me when I complimented you. You used to always argue with anyone who tried to compliment you. Faith, you've changed. What's up, girl? Talk to me."

"Oh, the usual. I fell in love with a man I can never have. But someone I've waited a lifetime to find. That's all." She didn't try to hide the wistful note in her voice.

"Oh, no. That's not even close to being all. Come on, Faith, talk to me," Jan insisted.

So Faith shared with her friend everything that had happened to her since they'd last seen each other. She told Jan how much she loved Edward. She told her how Edward had taught her to take a compliment, and to stop putting herself down. Without going into too much detail, she told Jan of the times that Edward had held her and kissed her.

"And, Jan, even though I know he doesn't love me, I do believe that he found me attractive. I'm convinced of that now, because of some of his actions—and reactions," she added with an embarrassed smile. "So, if I can cause that kind of reaction from a man like Edward Brenner, then I must not be all bad. I'm really trying to make myself think only positive things about myself, now. When I look in the mirror and the old negative thoughts start trying to resurface, about how bad I look, I just make myself stop thinking those thoughts and remind myself that Edward said I was beautiful. And that he wanted me." Here she stopped and giggled like a schoolgirl. "So, I try to concentrate on my best features, and I realize now I do have some pretty good features." Faith ended her speech with a big smile.

"Honey, who has always tried to tell you that you're beautiful?" Jan was pointing at herself as she asked the question.

"I know," Faith admitted, "but it's easier to believe a stranger, especially if that stranger is a handsome man, than a friend who loves you unconditionally."

"Well, just promise me that you won't change back. I really dig this new acceptance you have of yourself." Then as an afterthought, Jan moaned.

"What?" Faith asked.

"I'll never get a man to look at me if you keep strutting around like you did when we came into this restaurant. Every man in here was staring at you."

"Why, thank you," Faith said, smiling her biggest smile.

"Oooohhhhh." Again Jan moaned. "I'm afraid Edward Brenner has created a monster."

The two friends laughed, and suddenly Faith felt better.

**Three weeks had passed since Faith had left Edward and Mississippi.** She'd returned to her old job without any difficulty, and kept hoping she'd start to feel at home back in her old routine.

She sat looking at the house around her. It held no attraction for her anymore. Living alone had become a lonely routine for her. She scolded herself daily for even hoping to hear from Edward. He'd probably make arrangements for the divorce without even contacting her. She'd just receive the divorce papers in the mail one day.

She was startled out of her morbid thoughts by an abrupt movement in her stomach. She'd thought the fluttering and unnatural movements in her stomach would disappear after she got home and settled down a little, but they seemed to be getting worse, and this one was really unusual feeling. And her clothes were feeling tighter around the waist, as if she were swollen. It was time to see her doctor and see what was going on.

The next morning found her in her most hated position—on the examining table at Dr. Lambert's office. Dr. Lambert had been her doctor for several years, and she really liked him, but that didn't make this type of examination any more pleasant. He'd been the doctor who had told her she was pregnant after her ill-fated night with Frank Brenner.

Finally the doctor stood and wrote a few words on Faith's chart before turning back to face her and the accompanying nurse. There was an obvious twinkle in his kindly blue eyes, and Faith immediately felt better. Surely he wouldn't be close to laughing if something horrid were wrong with her.

"Well, little lady, I'm disappointed that I haven't seen you in here before now, but the baby seems to be doing fine. You look to be about four and a half months pregnant by now, but I want to hook you up with a regular obstetrician. As you know, I don't specialize in births, and I'd feel better if you were with a specialist, under the circumstances of your conception."

Faith could only stare at the doctor with her mouth gaping open, trying to comprehend what he had said.

"Faith? Are you okay?" His words finally penetrated her stunned mind.

"But Doctor Lambert, they said I'd lost the baby," she whispered, still in shock.

"Who said that? Faith, you aren't making any sense. What are you talking about? Here, sit up and drape this sheet around yourself and talk to me."

As briefly as possible, Faith told the doctor about her marriage to Edward, about the wreck they'd had, and the ensuing loss of feeling in her legs.

"Why didn't you tell me about all of this before I examined you?" Faith sensed the mild reprimand in his voice.

"I didn't think it had anything to do with my present situation," she shrugged.

"Well, don't try to second guess these things in the future, okay? You need to be upfront and honest with me, and any other doctor, if you want us to be able to help you. Now there are two possibilities here. The people at the hospital who said you'd lost the baby could have been mistaken. But, and this is my guess, you may have been pregnant with twins, and just lost one of them."

"How could that happen?"

"Well, occasionally two separate eggs become fertilized, but for some reason one will abort and the other one will stay. I highly suspect that's what happened with you. At any rate, you *are* pregnant, and you need to be under constant doctor's care."

**Back at home, Faith stared into space as she sat and tried to soak in this newfound truth.** She was pregnant! This time the news didn't devastate her like it had before. In fact, the more she thought about it, the more excited she became. Now she'd have something tangible to remind her of Edward. This baby might be his brother's child, but it still had Edward's blood running through its veins, and that was close enough.

Now she didn't have to face the future alone. She would have a baby to love her unconditionally, as only a baby can love. She would have someone to come home to at night. Someone to talk to and share her love with.

Suddenly her life had meaning, and she couldn't keep the happy smile from spreading across her face.

Her joyful moment was ripped open by the shrill intrusion of the doorbell. *Who could this be?* she wondered impatiently. She wasn't expecting anyone.

She opened the door and looked into the clear blue eyes of Edward Brenner.

"I've come to talk about our divorce, Mrs. Brenner."

Warring emotions engulfed Faith, causing her throat to try to close up on her. She wanted nothing more than to throw her arms around Edward and tell him how much she loved him, and that Frank's baby still lived, or at least one of them. Yet here he stood telling her he wanted a divorce.

She stepped numbly aside and motioned for him to enter. "Would you like some coffee?" she asked, not looking directly at him.

"Yes, that would be nice," he answered, devouring her with his eyes.

What would he say if he found out she was still pregnant? she wondered, as she went to the kitchen to make the coffee. And, instantly, she knew he must never know the truth. It would only put them back in the same situation they'd been in before.

"Aren't you just a little glad to see me?" Edward asked from the doorway.

Faith carefully poured water into the coffee maker, and then gripped the counter top until her knuckles turned white. She felt hot tears burn the inside of her eyelids. Slowly she turned to face him.

He stood with his arms crossed across his chest, leaning against the frame of the door, watching her. Her heart pounded so hard against her ribcage she could see her clothes vibrating in her peripheral vision.

She couldn't fake it any longer. What did it matter, anyway? He'd said he'd come to get the divorce, so what did it matter if he knew how she felt? Her feelings for him couldn't change anything now. He probably had the divorce papers in his pocket.

"Glad to see you?" she asked in a voice barely audible. "Glad to see the man I will always love, arrive to hand me divorce papers? Glad to see the face I will see in my dreams for the rest of my life, but know I can't have? Glad to see the man who taught me how to love and accept myself, only to know that he will never love me like I want to be loved? No, Edward, I can't say that I'm glad to see you, under the circumstances." Her voice was trembling.

Several long strides brought him close, and he gripped the counter on each side of her. "Jan said this might be difficult, and I guess she was right."

He was so close his breath fanned her hair.

"Jan? You've been talking to Jan? She double-crossed me!"

"No, she acted like a friend should act. She called and told me she had a friend who was having a hard time getting over her marriage."

As he talked, he took her face between his hands. "Faith, look at me," he implored.

When she looked into his eyes she saw a burning that she had seen before, but now it was even brighter than it had ever been.

"Faith, I have loved you ever since the day we stood before that old minister and I promised to love you and cherish you, for better or for worse, through good times and bad, until death do us part. As I told you once before, that promise I made was from the heart when I made it, and it's even more so now. Baby, I love you. I don't want a divorce. I was already planning to come here and try to talk you out of it, when Jan called and told me you were in love with me. Please tell me it's true. Please tell me all the things I just thought I heard you say are true. Do you really love me? I was crazy when I came home that night and found your note, and I've been crazy these past weeks without you. Tell me what I desperately want to hear."

"It's true," Faith answered, barely able to breathe, afraid to believe she'd heard Edward correctly.

"Then say it again," he persisted. "Make me believe it."

"Oh, Edward, I think I've loved you from the beginning, too. I love you, I love you, I love—"

His lips silenced her words.

When he finally ended the kiss, Faith slumped weakly against his chest. "Edward?" Her voice was barely more than a whisper, and a sob caught in her throat.

"What's wrong?" he asked, pulling away enough to look at her face, and seeing the concern there.

"I—I went to the doctor today, and I'm still pregnant with Frank's child."

"What? But how can that be?"

She told him what the doctor had said, watching his face as she talked.

"How do you feel about that?" His voice was guarded.

"Oh, Edward. I was so afraid and alone when I left you and came home. My life wasn't worth anything to me anymore. Then when I found out I was pregnant today, I was so excited. I finally realized how sad I'd been at the thought of losing my baby, even if it was conceived under bad circumstances. I'm so glad I didn't lose our baby."

Again Edward gathered her close and lowered his lips to hers. His kisses had always been tender, but this kiss was so gentle Faith could feel her throat aching from the love she could feel pouring from him into her very soul.

Her arms slid around his neck and she buried her fingers in his dark hair. She reveled in the freedom she suddenly felt to love him openly, as she had done so many times in her dreams. She melded her body to his and returned his kiss, trying to relay the love she felt for him.

His voice was ragged with emotion as he pulled away from her and asked, "Does this mean the divorce is off?"

"You better believe it! You blew your only chance for freedom!" She gloried in her newfound confidence.

"Then could we possibly consummate this marriage we're not going to end?"

"You mean right now?" Her earlier confidence wavered slightly, as shyness overcame her.

"Yes, right now," Edward said. "I've waited and dreamed about this moment long enough."

The gurgling and spitting of the coffee pot, signaling the coffee was done, momentarily caught Faith's attention.

"But what about the coffee?" she asked, feeling ridiculous as soon as the words left her mouth.

"Forget the coffee, baby. You have something I want much more than coffee," he whispered against her lips.

# *About the Author*

**Pat Ballard lives in Nashville, TN.** She writes motivational romance novels with Big Beautiful Heroines to show that plus-size women can be just as sexy, romantic, and exciting as their slim sisters.

Visit Pat at www.patballard.com.

**Check out other books by Pat—and more—at the Pearlsong Press website at www.pearlsong.com.**

www.ingramcontent.com/pod-product-compliance
Lightning Source LLC
Chambersburg PA
CBHW052137170626
46812CB00004B/1468
*9780971324770*